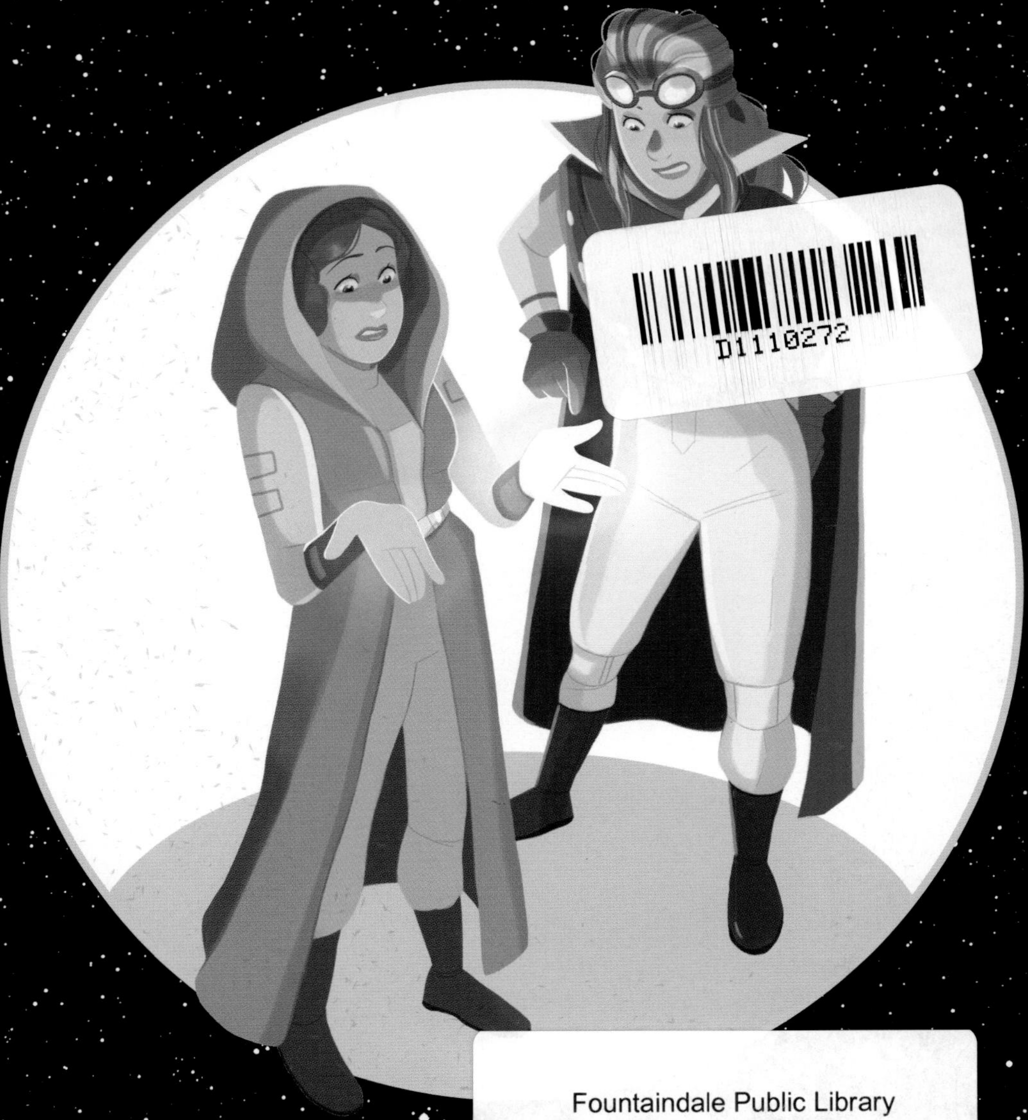

STAR WARS™ ADVENTURES

DRIVING FORCE

Facebook: **facebook.com/idwpublishing**
Twitter: **@idwpublishing**
YouTube: **youtube.com/idwpublishing**
Tumblr: **tumblr.idwpublishing.com**
Instagram: **instagram.com/idwpublishing**

ISBN: 978-1-68405-715-3   23 22 21 20   1 2 3 4

COVER ARTIST
MEGAN LEVENS

COVER COLORIST
CHARLIE KIRCHOFF

LETTERER
TOM B. LONG

SERIES ASSISTANT EDITOR
ELIZABETH BREI

SERIES EDITOR
DENTON J. TIPTON

COLLECTION EDITORS
ALONZO SIMON
& ZAC BOONE

COLLECTION DESIGNER
CLYDE GRAPA

STAR WARS ADVENTURES, VOLUME 10: DRIVING FORCE.
SEPTEMBER 2020. FIRST PRINTING. © 2020 Lucasfilm Ltd. &
® or ™ where indicated. All Rights Reserved. © 2020 Idea
and Design Works, LLC. The IDW logo is registered in the U.S.
Patent and Trademark Office. IDW Publishing, a division of Idea
and Design Works, LLC. Editorial offices: 2765 Truxtun Road,
San Diego, CA 92106. Any similarities to persons living or dead
are purely coincidental. With the exception of artwork used for
review purposes, none of the contents of this publication may be
reprinted without the permission of Idea and Design Works, LLC.
Printed in Korea.
IDW Publishing does not read or accept unsolicited submissions of
ideas, stories, or artwork.

Originally published as STAR WARS ADVENTURES issues #24–26.

Chris Ryall, President & Publisher/CCO
Cara Morrison, Chief Financial Officer
Matthew Ruzicka, Chief Accounting Officer
John Barber, Editor-in-Chief
Justin Eisinger, Editorial Director, Graphic Novels and Collections
Jerry Bennington, VP of New Product Development
Lorelei Bunjes, VP of Technology & Information Services
Jud Meyers, Sales Director
Anna Morrow, Marketing Director
Tara McCrillis, Director of Design & Production
Mike Ford, Director of Operations
Shauna Monteforte, Manufacturing Operations Director
Rebekah Cahalin, General Manager

Ted Adams and Robbie Robbins, IDW Founders

Lucasfilm Credits:
Robert Simpson, Senior Editor
Michael Siglain, Creative Director
Phil Szostak, Lucasfilm Art Department
Matt Martin, Pablo Hidalgo, and
Emily Shkoukani, Story Group

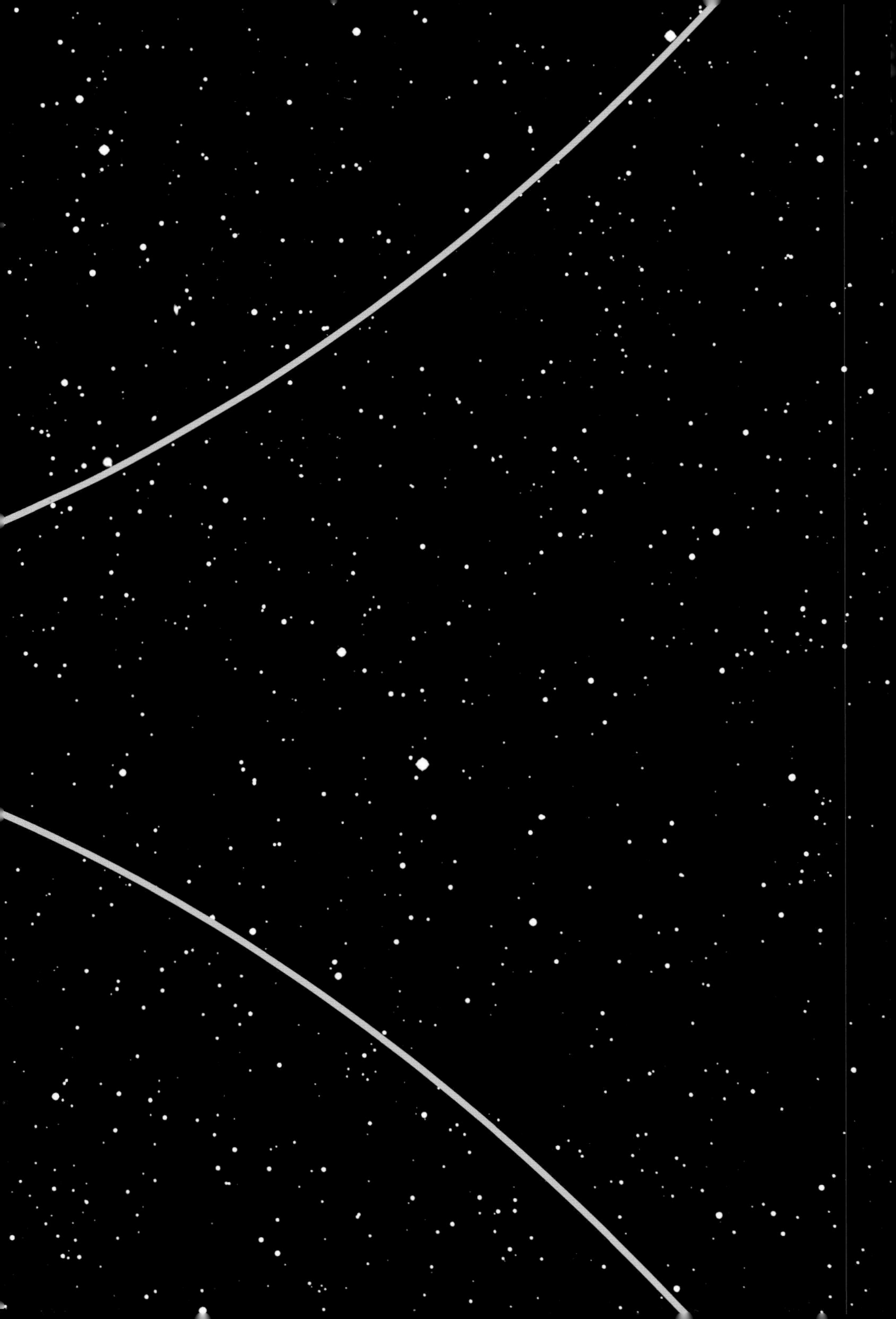

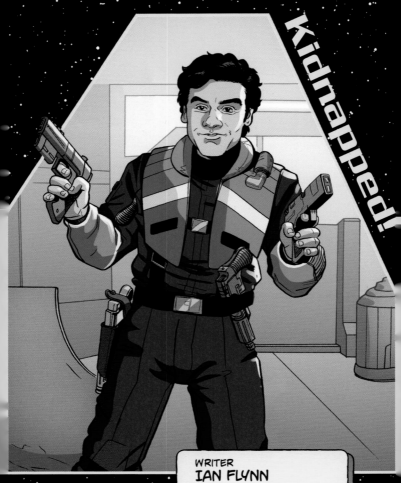

STAR WARS ADVENTURES

Kidnapped!

WRITER
IAN FLYNN

ARTIST
MEGAN LEVENS

COLORIST
CHARLIE KIRCHOFF

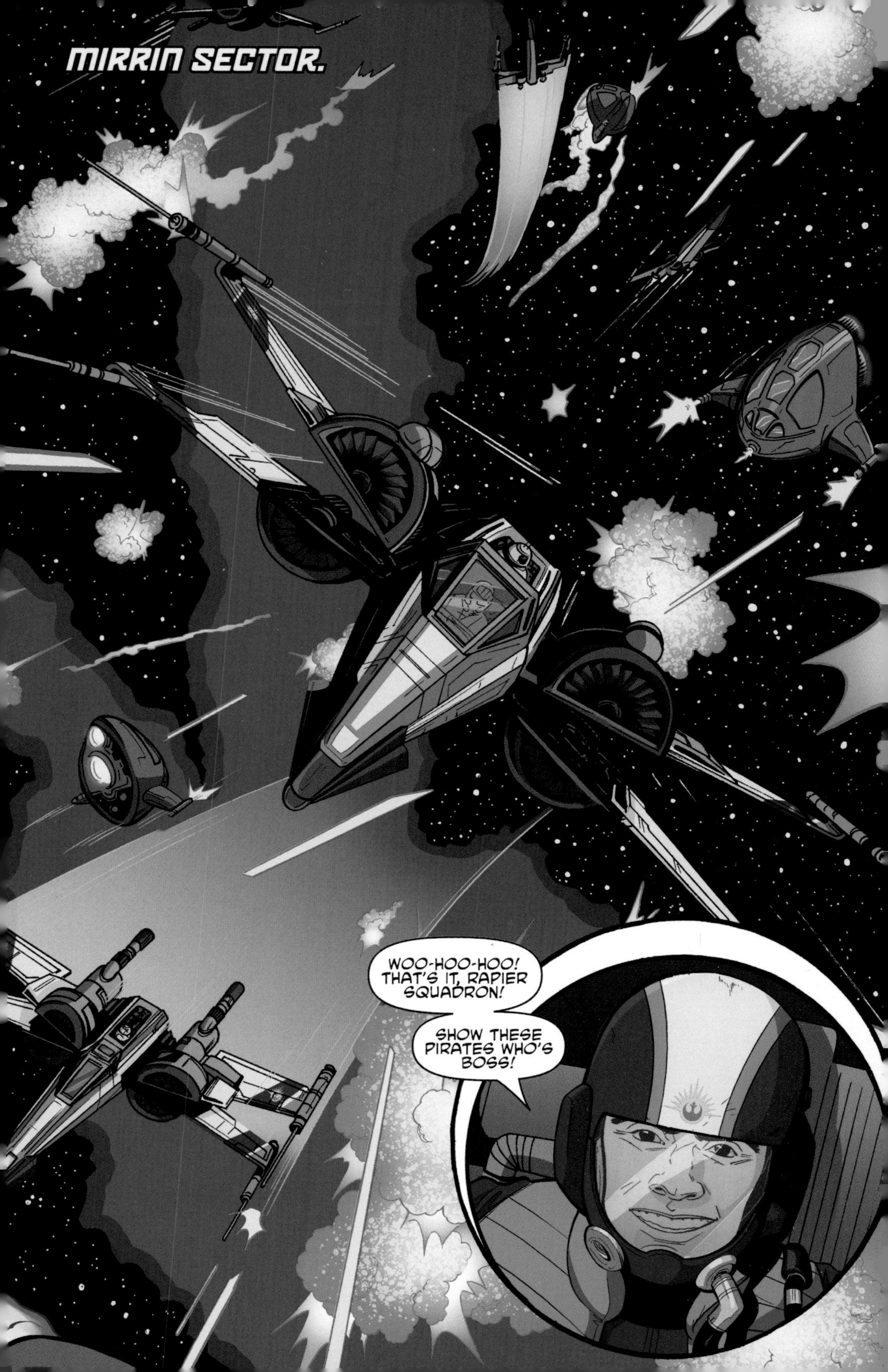
MIRRIN SECTOR.
WOO-HOO-HOO! THAT'S IT, RAPIER SQUADRON!
SHOW THESE PIRATES WHO'S BOSS!

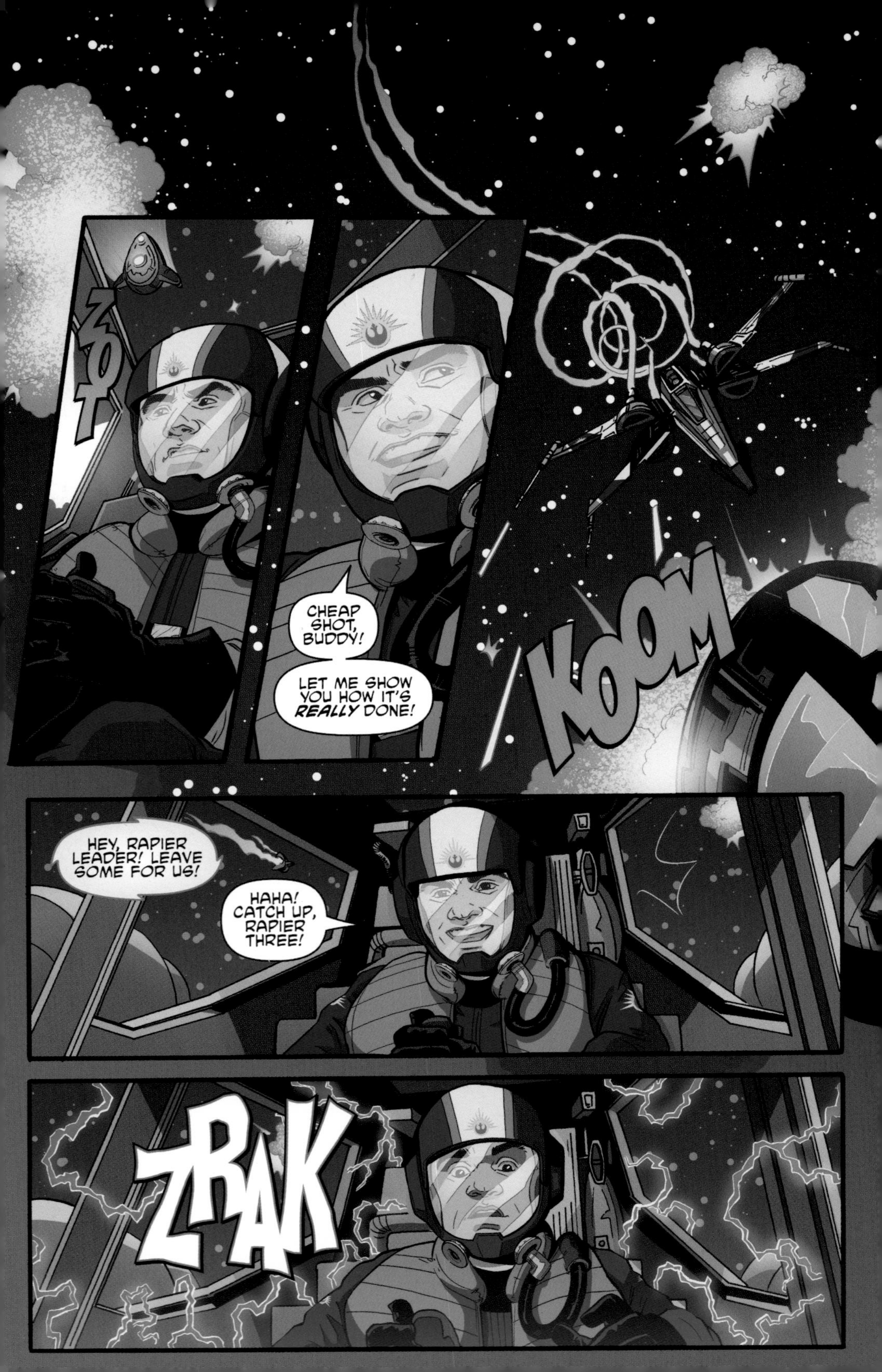
ZOT
CHEAP SHOT, BUDDY!
LET ME SHOW YOU HOW IT'S *REALLY* DONE!
KOOM
HEY, RAPIER LEADER! LEAVE SOME FOR US!
HAHA! CATCH UP, RAPIER THREE!
ZRAK

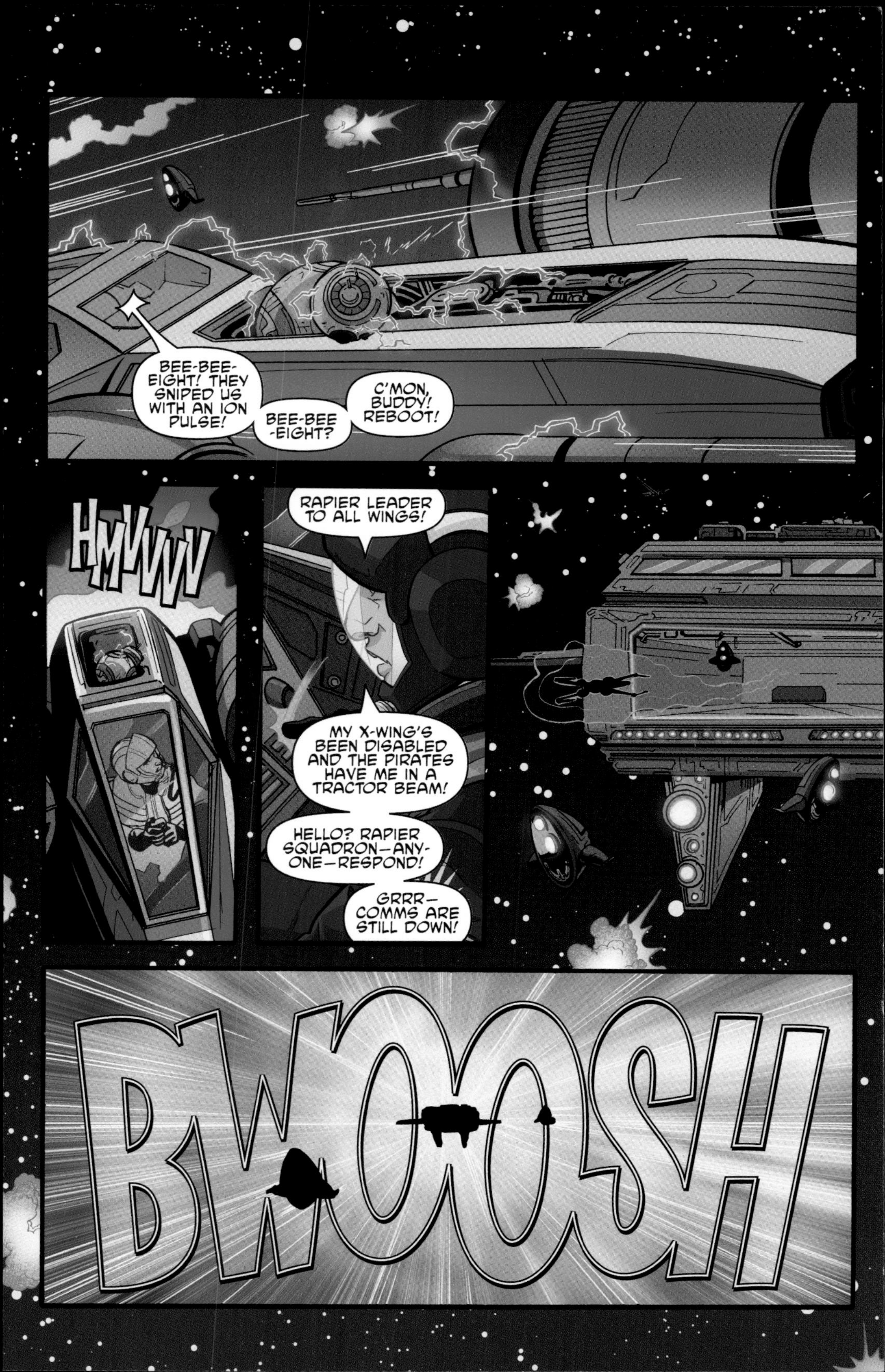
BEE-BEE-EIGHT! THEY SNIPED US WITH AN ION PULSE!
BEE-BEE-EIGHT?
C'MON, BUDDY! REBOOT!
HMVVVVV
RAPIER LEADER TO ALL WINGS!
MY X-WING'S BEEN DISABLED AND THE PIRATES HAVE ME IN A TRACTOR BEAM!
HELLO? RAPIER SQUADRON—ANY-ONE—RESPOND!
GRRR—COMMS ARE STILL DOWN!
BWOOOSH

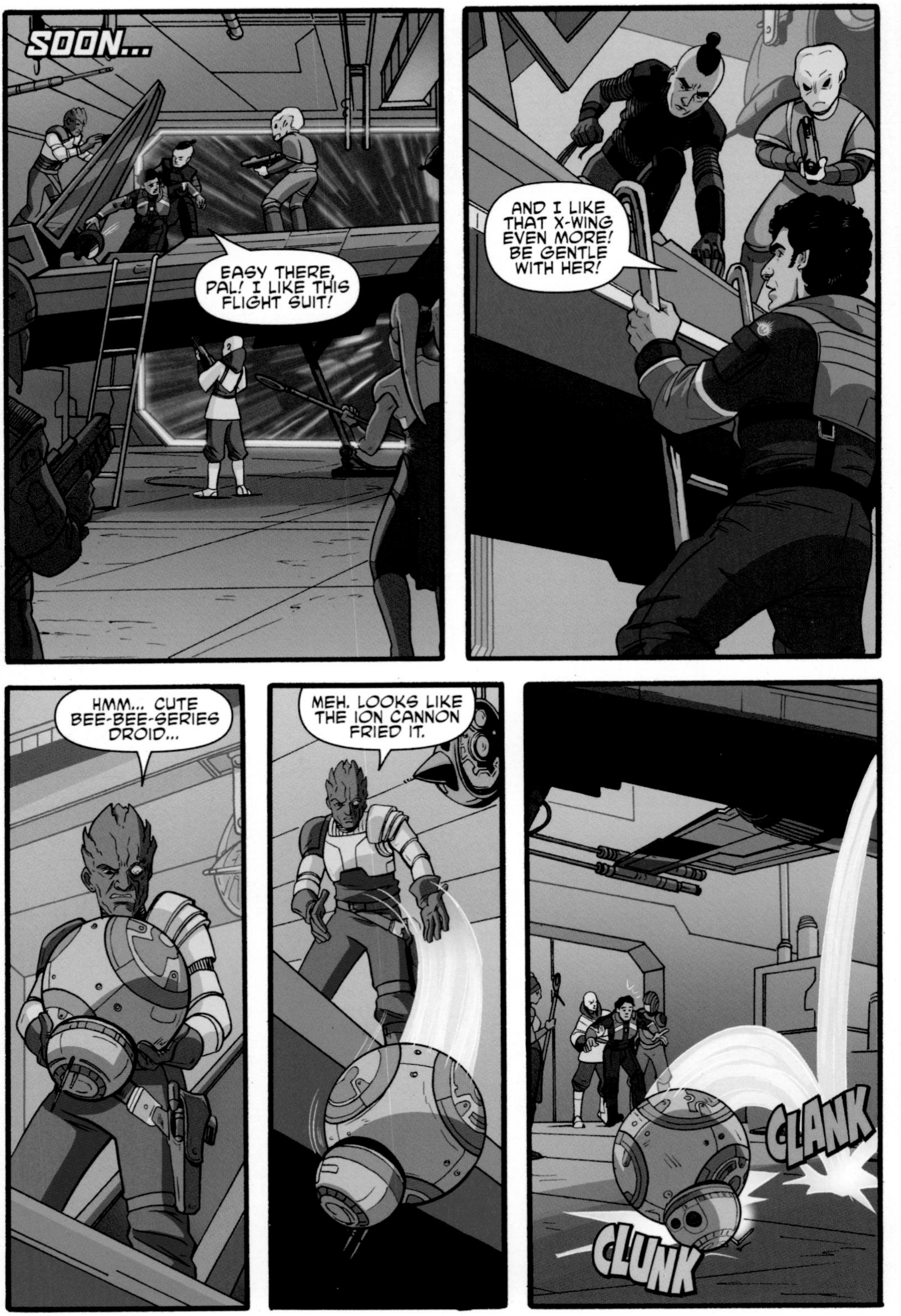
SOON...
EASY THERE, PAL! I LIKE THIS FLIGHT SUIT!
AND I LIKE THAT X-WING EVEN MORE! BE GENTLE WITH HER!
HMM... CUTE BEE-BEE-SERIES DROID...
MEH. LOOKS LIKE THE ION CANNON FRIED IT.
CLANK
CLUNK

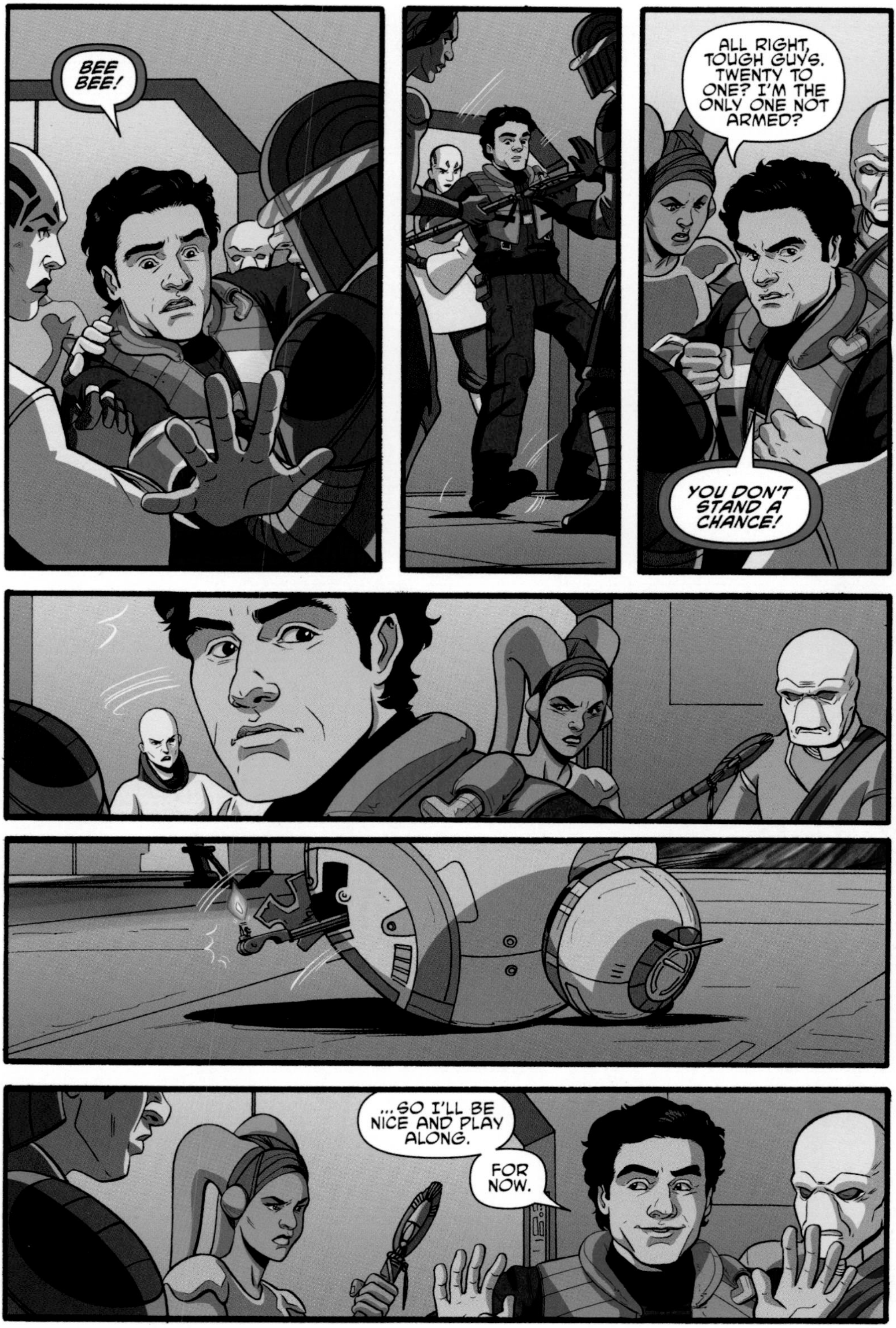
BEE BEE!
ALL RIGHT, TOUGH GUYS. TWENTY TO ONE? I'M THE ONLY ONE NOT ARMED?
YOU DON'T STAND A CHANCE!
...SO I'LL BE NICE AND PLAY ALONG.
FOR NOW.

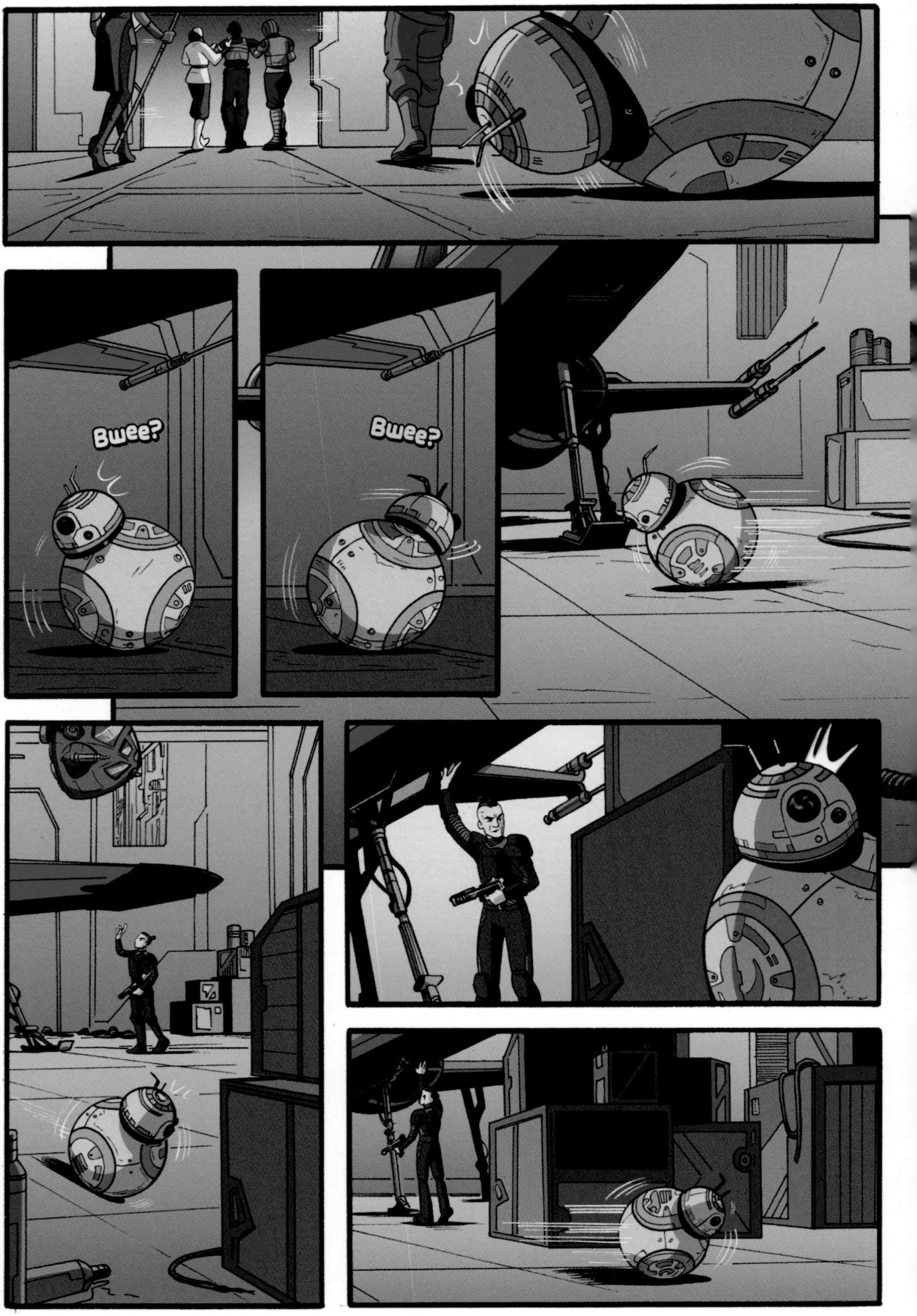
Bwee?
Bwee?

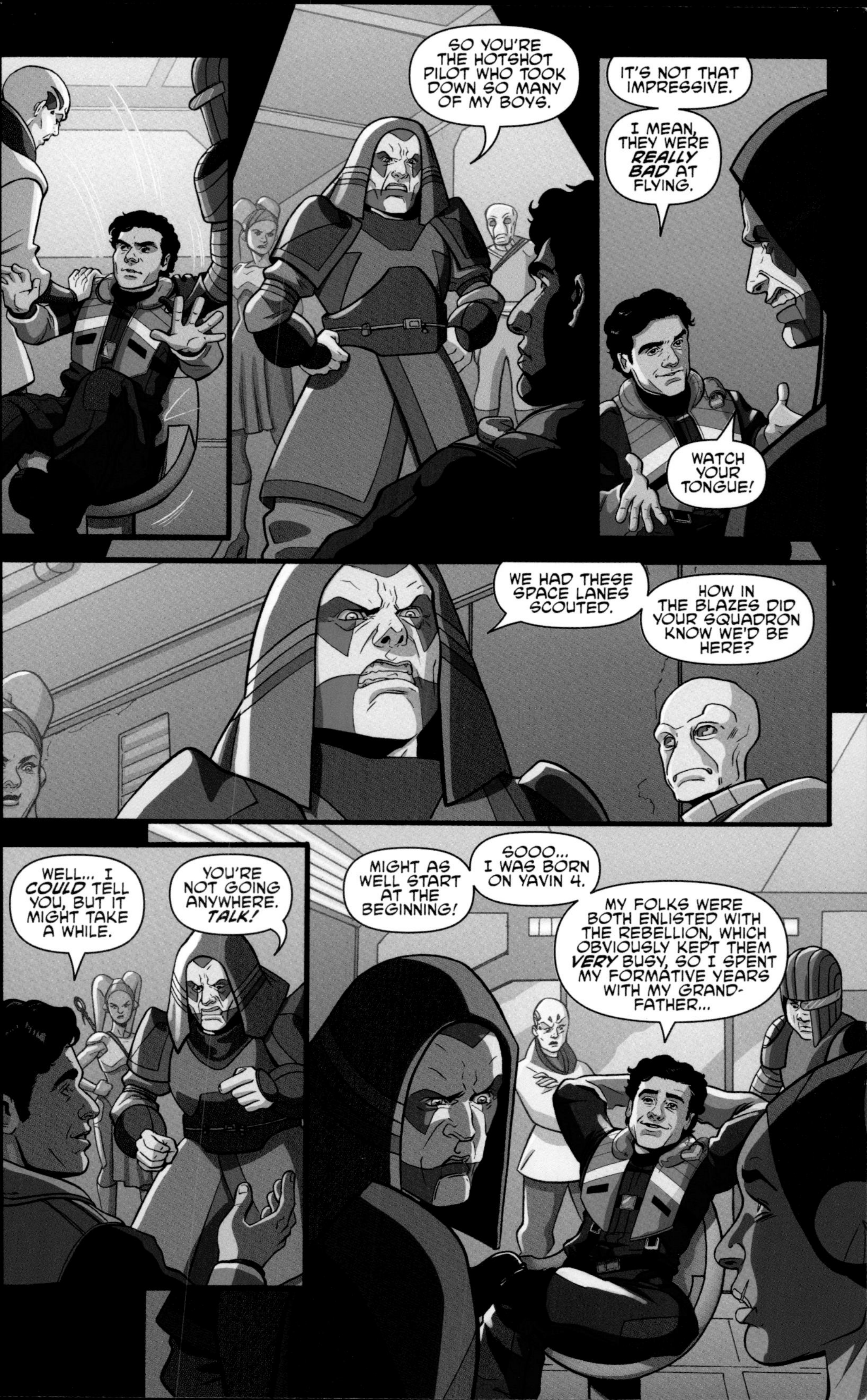
SO YOU'RE THE HOTSHOT PILOT WHO TOOK DOWN SO MANY OF MY BOYS.
IT'S NOT THAT IMPRESSIVE.
I MEAN, THEY WERE REALLY BAD AT FLYING.
WATCH YOUR TONGUE!
WE HAD THESE SPACE LANES SCOUTED.
HOW IN THE BLAZES DID YOUR SQUADRON KNOW WE'D BE HERE?
WELL... I COULD TELL YOU, BUT IT MIGHT TAKE A WHILE.
YOU'RE NOT GOING ANYWHERE. TALK!
MIGHT AS WELL START AT THE BEGINNING!
SOOO... I WAS BORN ON YAVIN 4.
MY FOLKS WERE BOTH ENLISTED WITH THE REBELLION, WHICH OBVIOUSLY KEPT THEM VERY BUSY, SO I SPENT MY FORMATIVE YEARS WITH MY GRAND-FATHER...

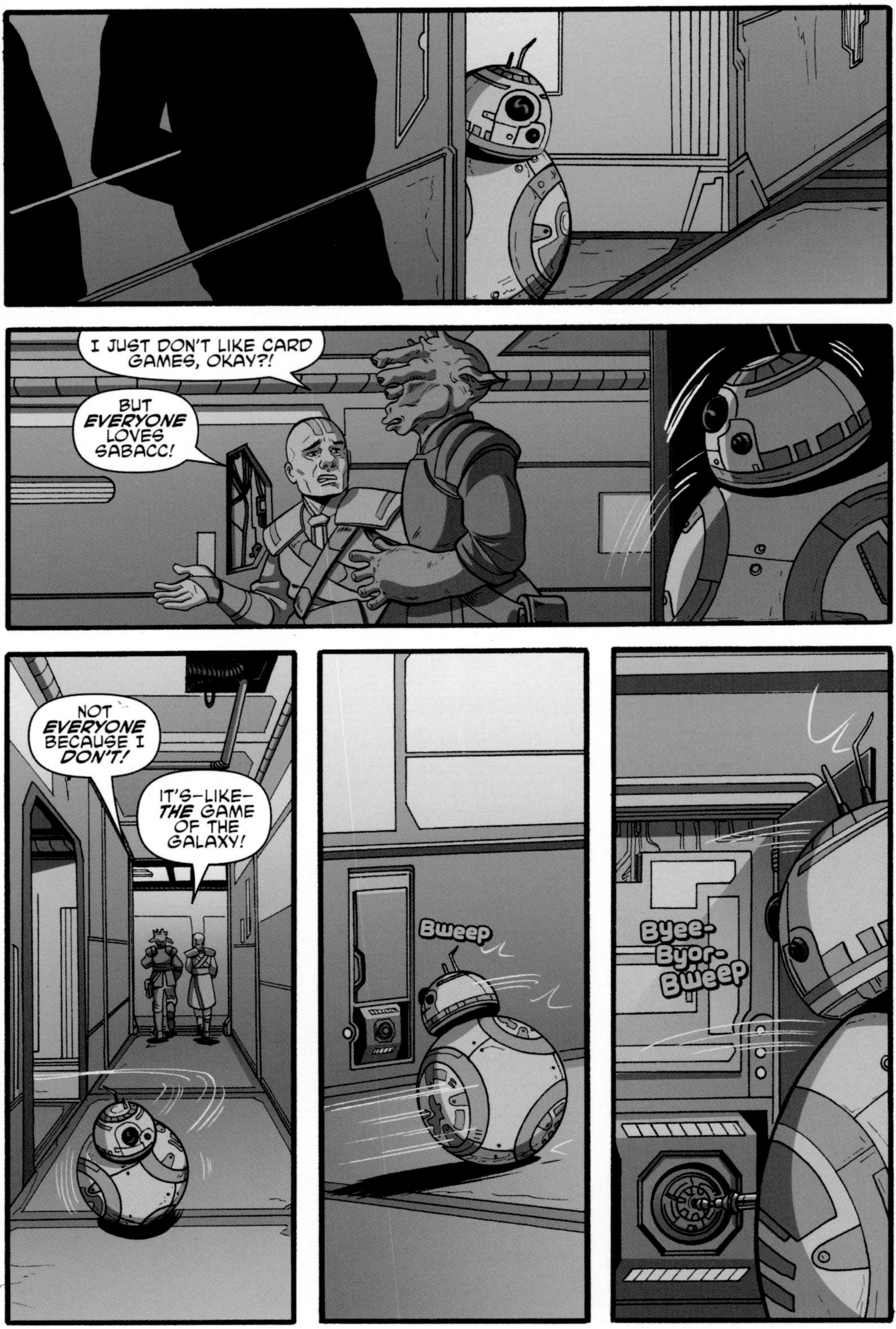
I JUST DON'T LIKE CARD GAMES, OKAY?!
BUT EVERYONE LOVES SABACC!
NOT EVERYONE BECAUSE I DON'T!
IT'S—LIKE—THE GAME OF THE GALAXY!
Bweep
Byee-Byor-Bweep

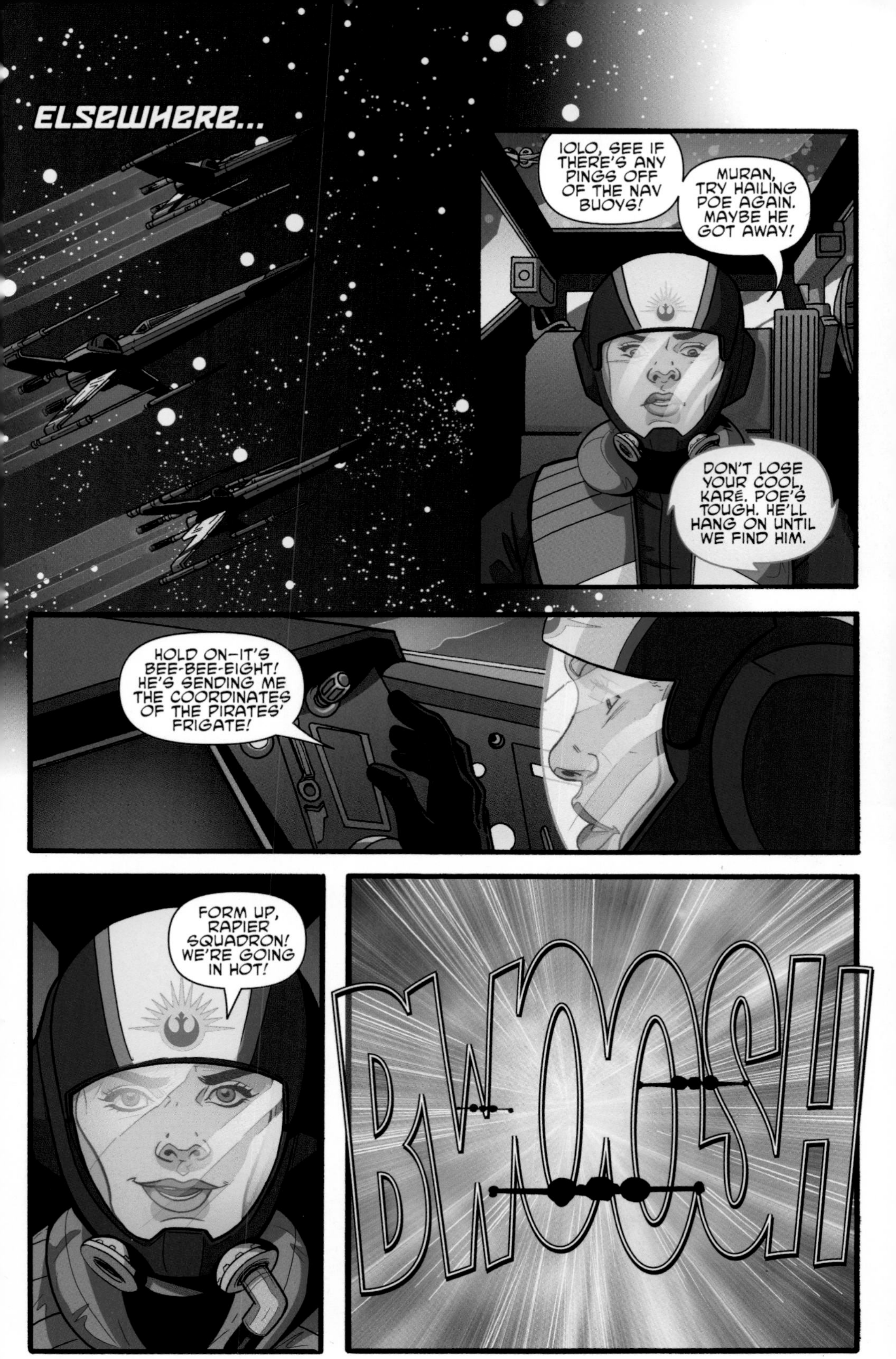
ELSEWHERE...
IOLO, SEE IF THERE'S ANY PINGS OFF OF THE NAV BUOYS!
MURAN, TRY HAILING POE AGAIN. MAYBE HE GOT AWAY!
DON'T LOSE YOUR COOL, KARÉ. POE'S TOUGH. HE'LL HANG ON UNTIL WE FIND HIM.
HOLD ON—IT'S BEE-BEE-EIGHT! HE'S SENDING ME THE COORDINATES OF THE PIRATES' FRIGATE!
FORM UP, RAPIER SQUADRON! WE'RE GOING IN HOT!
BWOOOSH

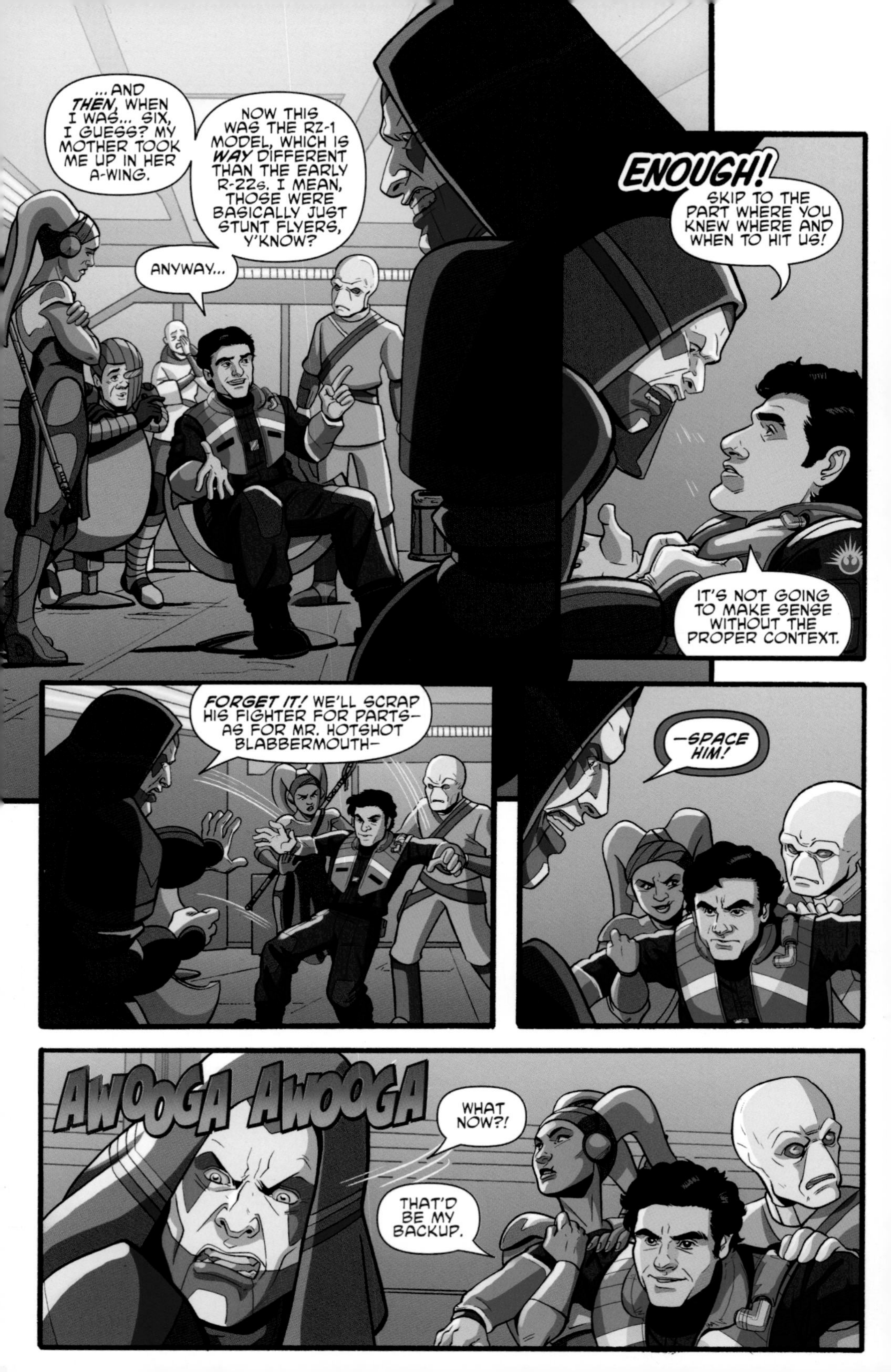
...AND THEN, WHEN I WAS... SIX, I GUESS? MY MOTHER TOOK ME UP IN HER A-WING.
NOW THIS WAS THE RZ-1 MODEL, WHICH IS WAY DIFFERENT THAN THE EARLY R-22s. I MEAN, THOSE WERE BASICALLY JUST STUNT FLYERS, Y'KNOW?
ANYWAY...
ENOUGH!
SKIP TO THE PART WHERE YOU KNEW WHERE AND WHEN TO HIT US!
IT'S NOT GOING TO MAKE SENSE WITHOUT THE PROPER CONTEXT.
FORGET IT! WE'LL SCRAP HIS FIGHTER FOR PARTS— AS FOR MR. HOTSHOT BLABBERMOUTH—
—SPACE HIM!
AWOOGA AWOOGA
WHAT NOW?!
THAT'D BE MY BACKUP.

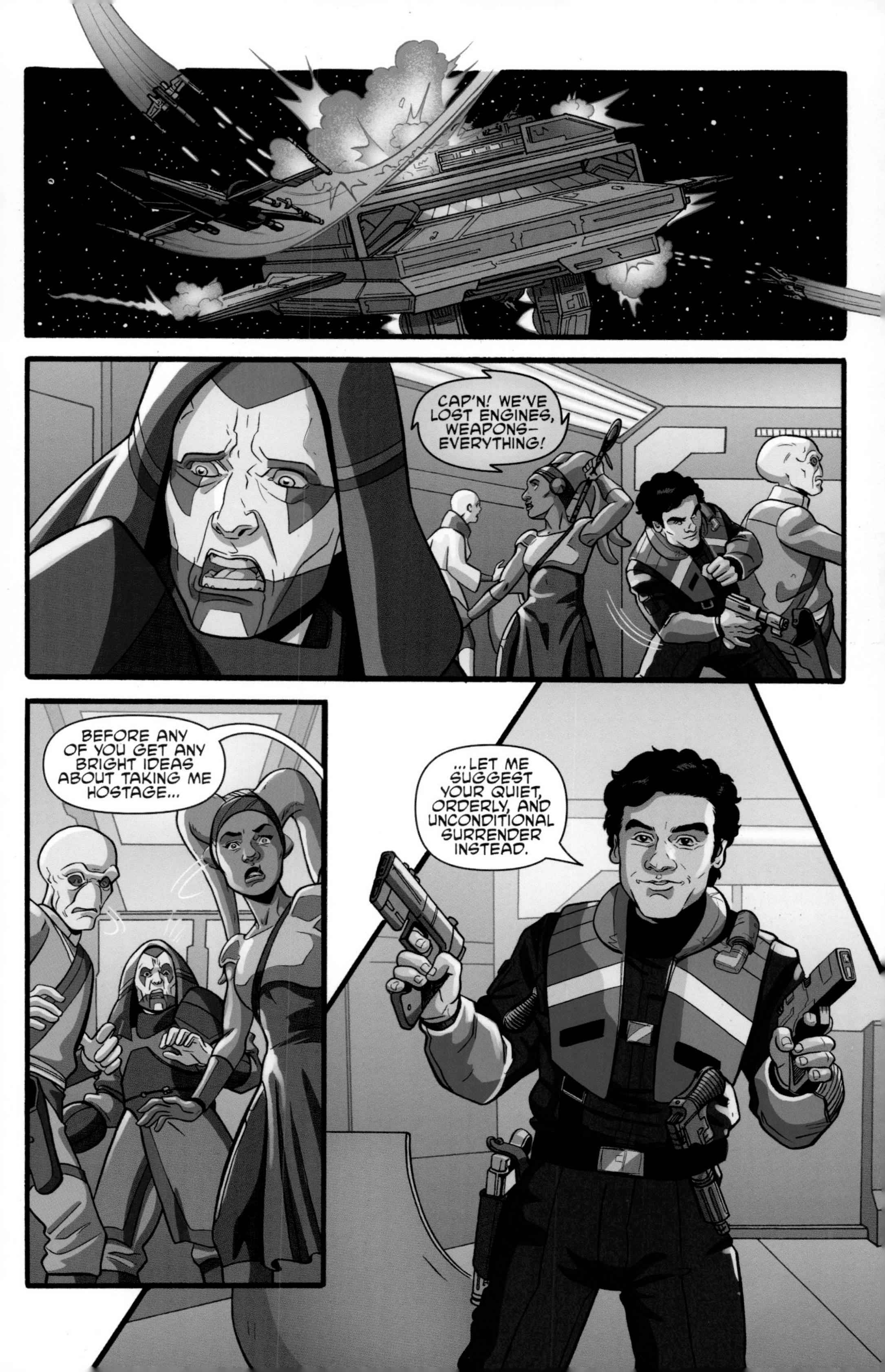
CAP'N! WE'VE LOST ENGINES, WEAPONS— EVERYTHING!
BEFORE ANY OF YOU GET ANY BRIGHT IDEAS ABOUT TAKING ME HOSTAGE...
...LET ME SUGGEST YOUR QUIET, ORDERLY, AND UNCONDITIONAL SURRENDER INSTEAD.

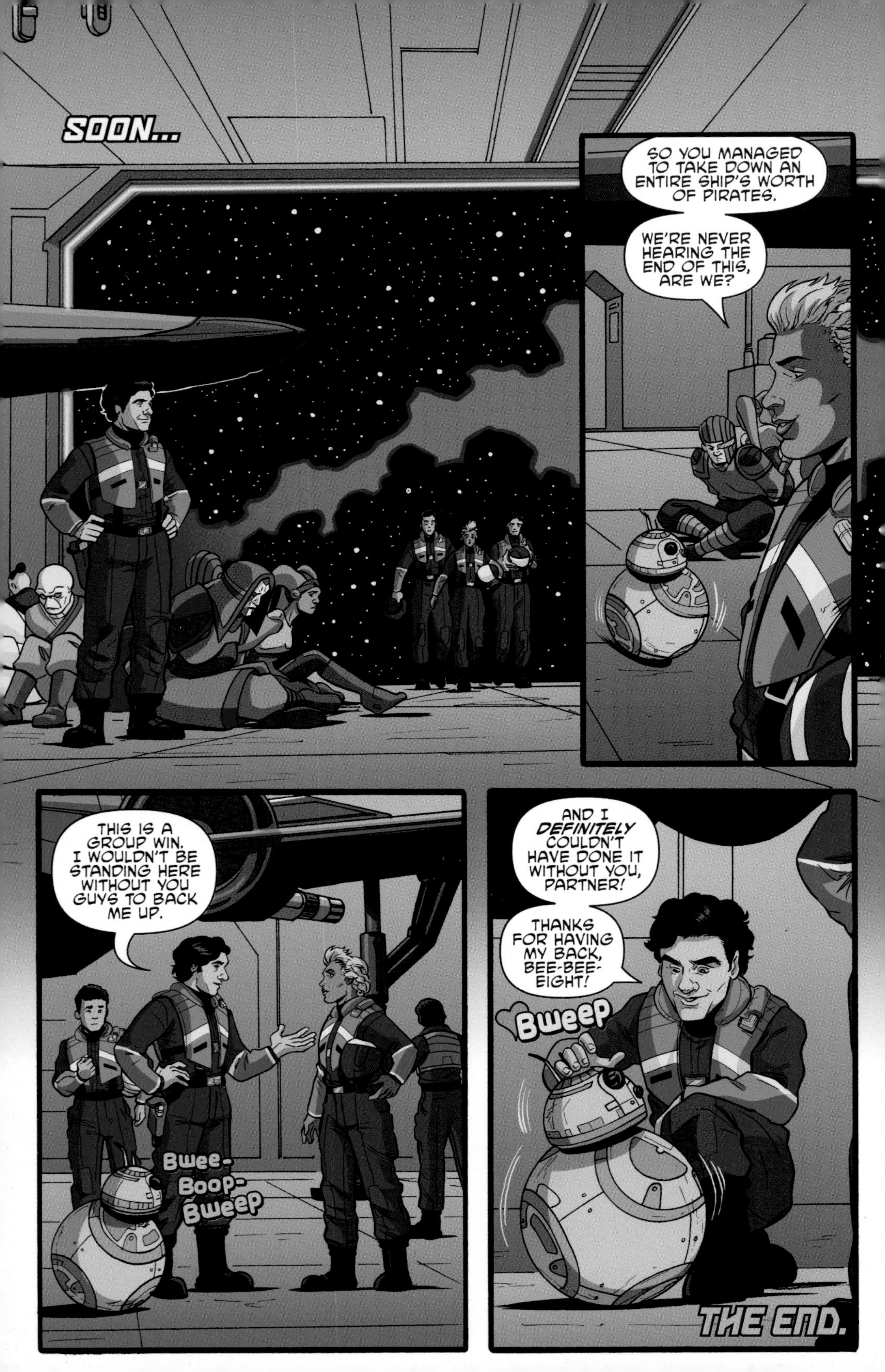
SOON...
SO YOU MANAGED TO TAKE DOWN AN ENTIRE SHIP'S WORTH OF PIRATES.
WE'RE NEVER HEARING THE END OF THIS, ARE WE?
THIS IS A GROUP WIN. I WOULDN'T BE STANDING HERE WITHOUT YOU GUYS TO BACK ME UP.
Bwee-Boop-Bweep
AND I *DEFINITELY* COULDN'T HAVE DONE IT WITHOUT YOU, PARTNER!
THANKS FOR HAVING MY BACK, BEE-BEE-EIGHT!
Bweep
THE END.

STAR WARS
—ADVENTURES—

The Right Wrong Turn

AHHHHHHH!

WRITER
DELILAH S. DAWSON

ARTIST
MARGAUX SALTEL

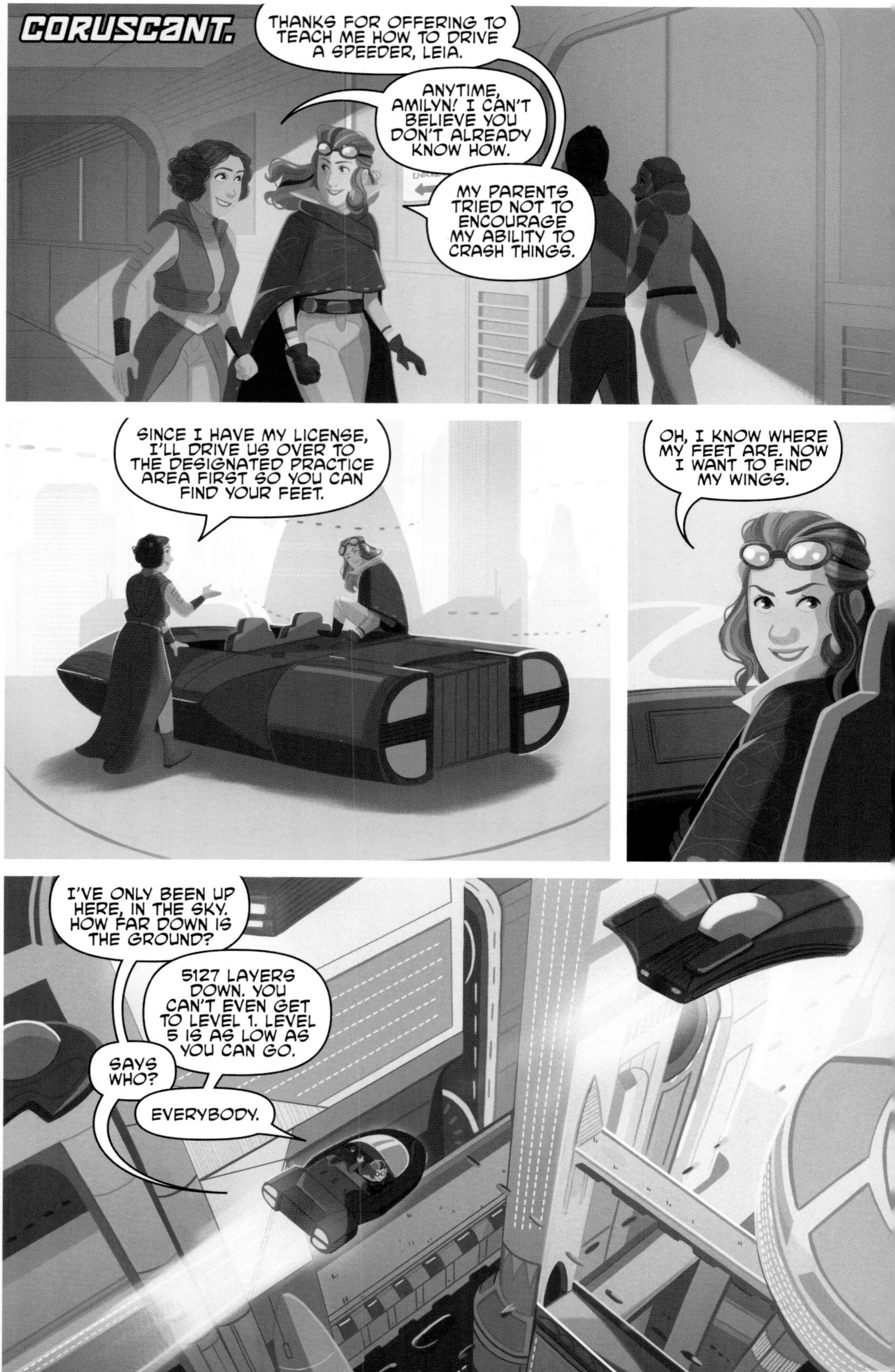
CORUSCANT.
THANKS FOR OFFERING TO TEACH ME HOW TO DRIVE A SPEEDER, LEIA.
ANYTIME, AMILYN! I CAN'T BELIEVE YOU DON'T ALREADY KNOW HOW.
MY PARENTS TRIED NOT TO ENCOURAGE MY ABILITY TO CRASH THINGS.
SINCE I HAVE MY LICENSE, I'LL DRIVE US OVER TO THE DESIGNATED PRACTICE AREA FIRST SO YOU CAN FIND YOUR FEET.
OH, I KNOW WHERE MY FEET ARE. NOW I WANT TO FIND MY WINGS.
I'VE ONLY BEEN UP HERE, IN THE SKY. HOW FAR DOWN IS THE GROUND?
5127 LAYERS DOWN. YOU CAN'T EVEN GET TO LEVEL 1. LEVEL 5 IS AS LOW AS YOU CAN GO.
SAYS WHO?
EVERYBODY.

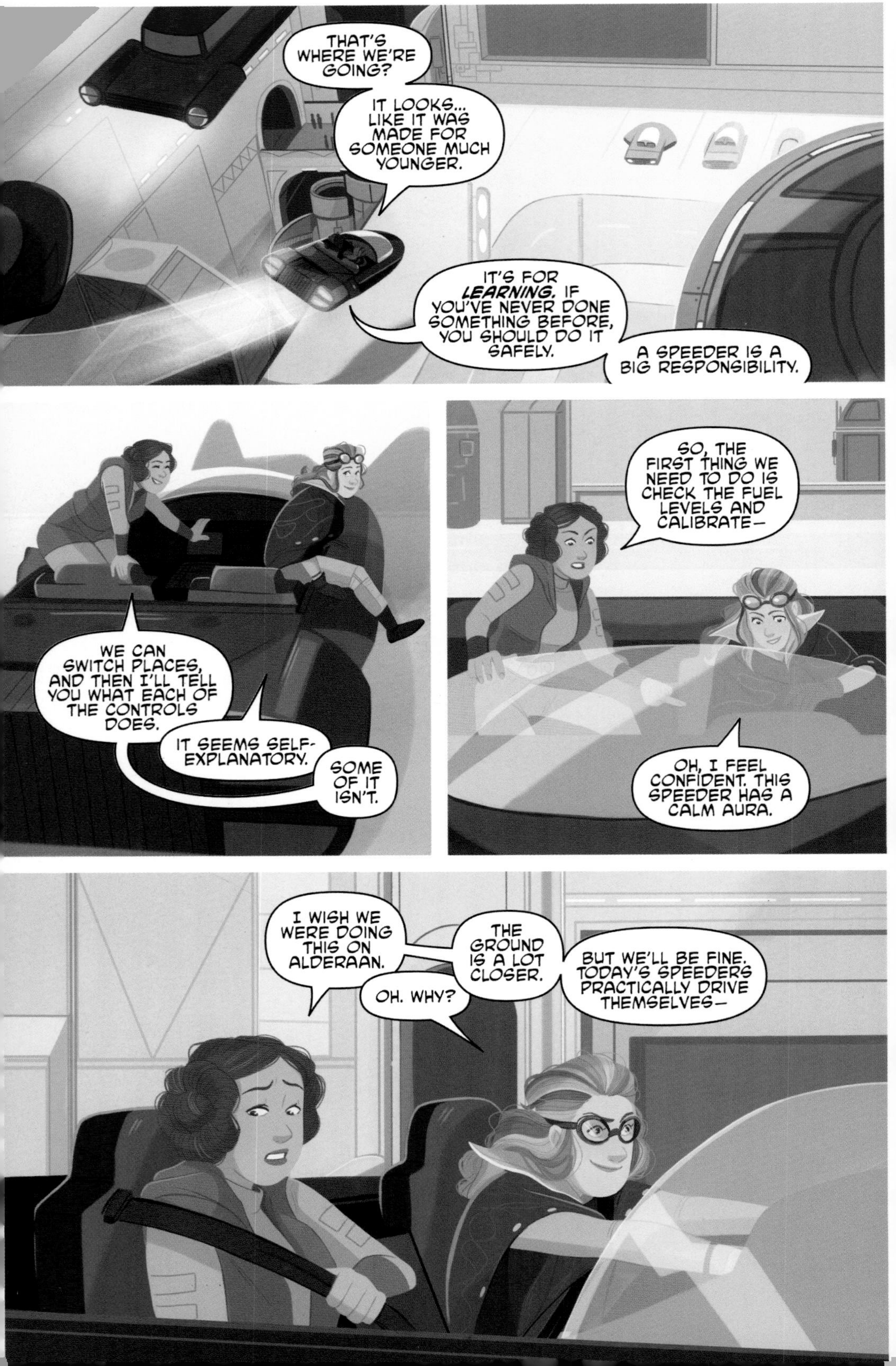
THAT'S WHERE WE'RE GOING?
IT LOOKS... LIKE IT WAS MADE FOR SOMEONE MUCH YOUNGER.
IT'S FOR *LEARNING.* IF YOU'VE NEVER DONE SOMETHING BEFORE, YOU SHOULD DO IT SAFELY.
A SPEEDER IS A BIG RESPONSIBILITY.
WE CAN SWITCH PLACES, AND THEN I'LL TELL YOU WHAT EACH OF THE CONTROLS DOES.
IT SEEMS SELF-EXPLANATORY.
SOME OF IT ISN'T.
SO, THE FIRST THING WE NEED TO DO IS CHECK THE FUEL LEVELS AND CALIBRATE—
OH, I FEEL CONFIDENT. THIS SPEEDER HAS A CALM AURA.
I WISH WE WERE DOING THIS ON ALDERAAN.
OH. WHY?
THE GROUND IS A LOT CLOSER.
BUT WE'LL BE FINE. TODAY'S SPEEDERS PRACTICALLY DRIVE THEMSELVES—

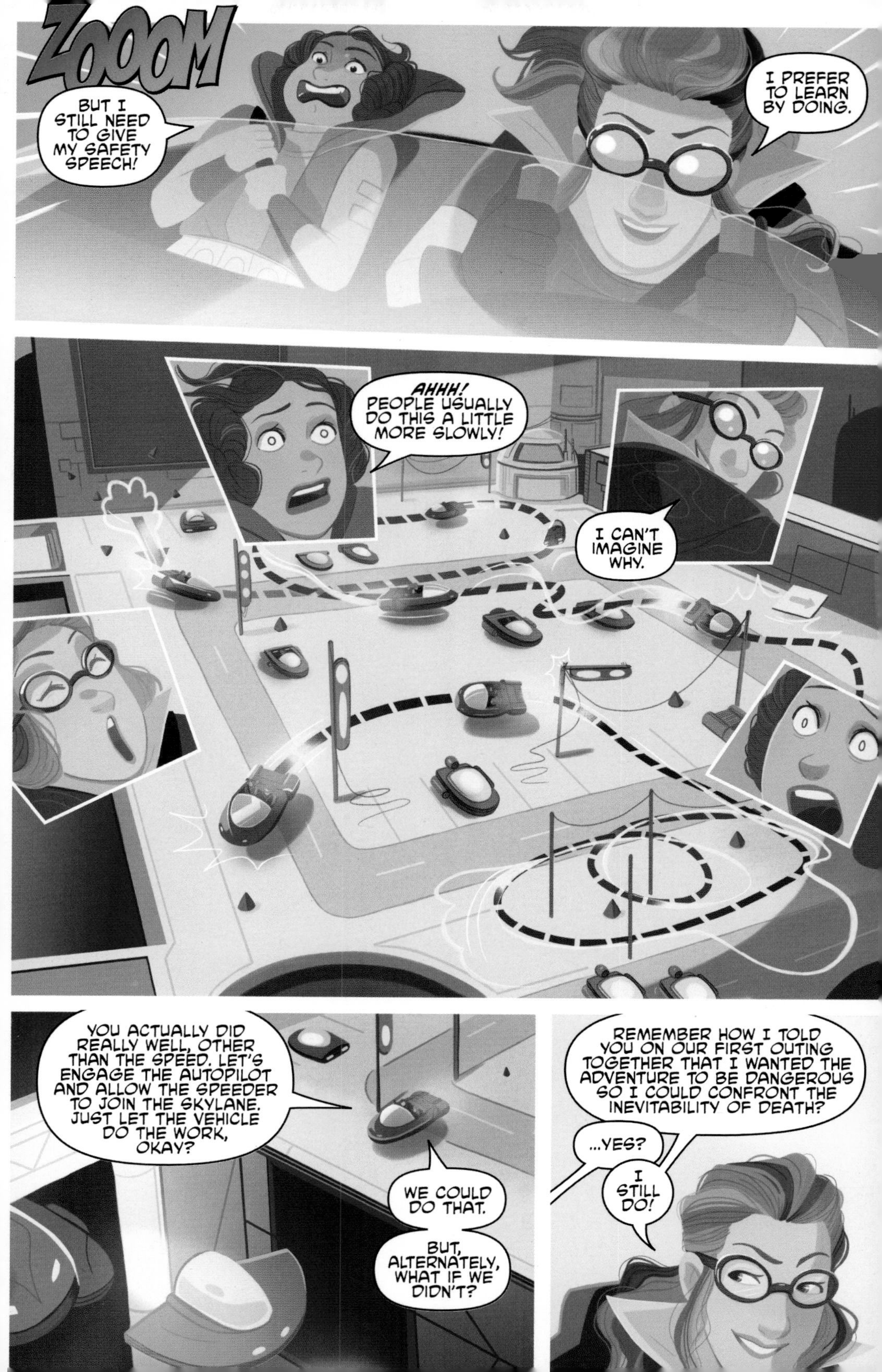
ZOOOM
BUT I STILL NEED TO GIVE MY SAFETY SPEECH!
I PREFER TO LEARN BY DOING.
AHHH! PEOPLE USUALLY DO THIS A LITTLE MORE SLOWLY!
I CAN'T IMAGINE WHY.
YOU ACTUALLY DID REALLY WELL, OTHER THAN THE SPEED. LET'S ENGAGE THE AUTOPILOT AND ALLOW THE SPEEDER TO JOIN THE SKYLANE. JUST LET THE VEHICLE DO THE WORK, OKAY?
WE COULD DO THAT.
BUT, ALTERNATELY, WHAT IF WE DIDN'T?
REMEMBER HOW I TOLD YOU ON OUR FIRST OUTING TOGETHER THAT I WANTED THE ADVENTURE TO BE DANGEROUS SO I COULD CONFRONT THE INEVITABILITY OF DEATH?
...YES?
I STILL DO!

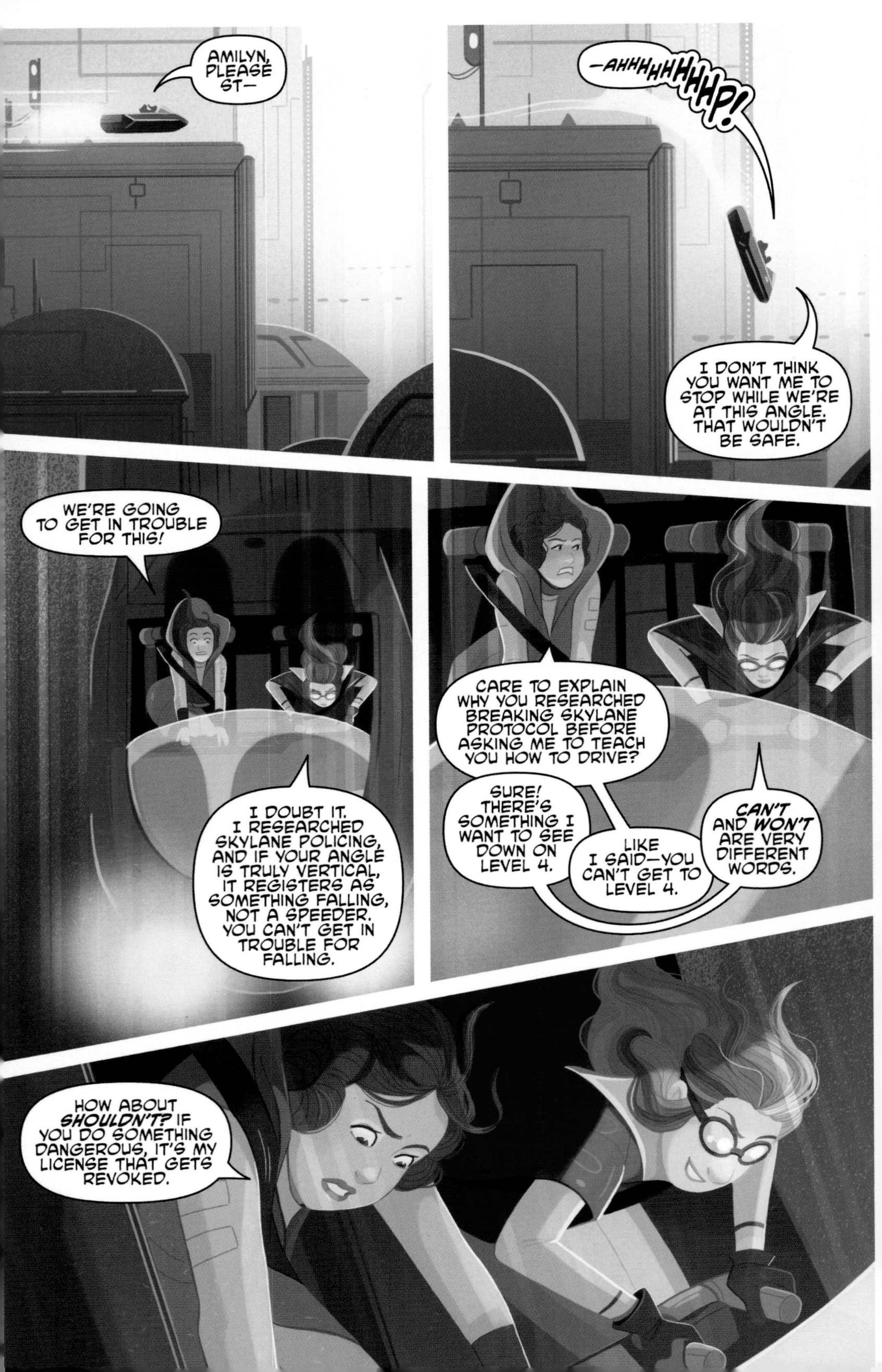
AMILYN, PLEASE ST—
—AHHHHHHHHP!
I DON'T THINK YOU WANT ME TO STOP WHILE WE'RE AT THIS ANGLE. THAT WOULDN'T BE SAFE.
WE'RE GOING TO GET IN TROUBLE FOR THIS!
I DOUBT IT. I RESEARCHED SKYLANE POLICING, AND IF YOUR ANGLE IS TRULY VERTICAL, IT REGISTERS AS SOMETHING FALLING, NOT A SPEEDER. YOU CAN'T GET IN TROUBLE FOR FALLING.
CARE TO EXPLAIN WHY YOU RESEARCHED BREAKING SKYLANE PROTOCOL BEFORE ASKING ME TO TEACH YOU HOW TO DRIVE?
SURE! THERE'S SOMETHING I WANT TO SEE DOWN ON LEVEL 4.
LIKE I SAID—YOU CAN'T GET TO LEVEL 4.
CAN'T AND *WON'T* ARE VERY DIFFERENT WORDS.
HOW ABOUT *SHOULDN'T?* IF YOU DO SOMETHING DANGEROUS, IT'S MY LICENSE THAT GETS REVOKED.

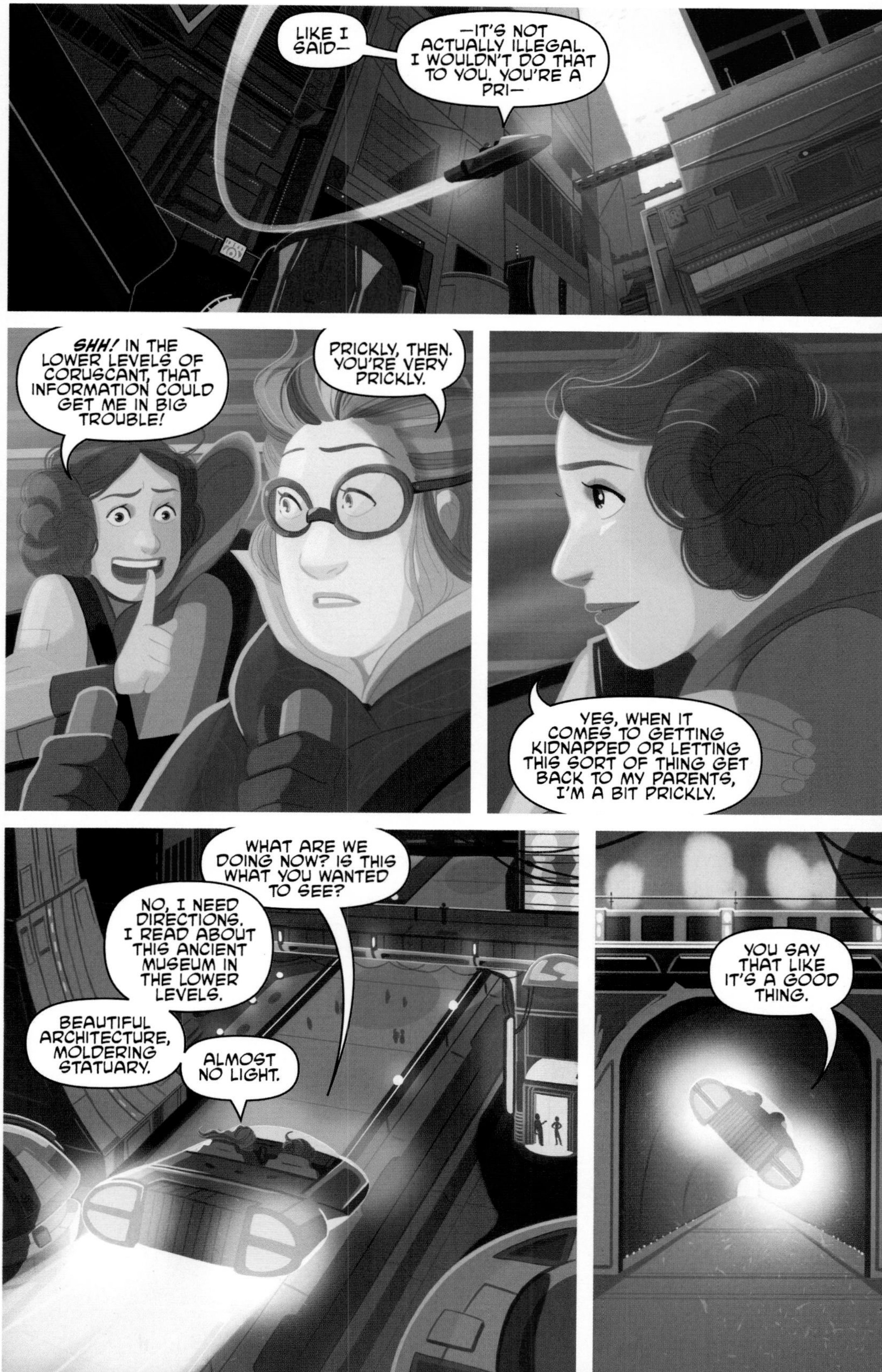
LIKE I SAID—
—IT'S NOT ACTUALLY ILLEGAL. I WOULDN'T DO THAT TO YOU. YOU'RE A PRI—
SHH! IN THE LOWER LEVELS OF CORUSCANT, THAT INFORMATION COULD GET ME IN BIG TROUBLE!
PRICKLY, THEN. YOU'RE VERY PRICKLY.
YES, WHEN IT COMES TO GETTING KIDNAPPED OR LETTING THIS SORT OF THING GET BACK TO MY PARENTS, I'M A BIT PRICKLY.
WHAT ARE WE DOING NOW? IS THIS WHAT YOU WANTED TO SEE?
NO, I NEED DIRECTIONS. I READ ABOUT THIS ANCIENT MUSEUM IN THE LOWER LEVELS.
BEAUTIFUL ARCHITECTURE, MOLDERING STATUARY.
ALMOST NO LIGHT.
YOU SAY THAT LIKE IT'S A GOOD THING.

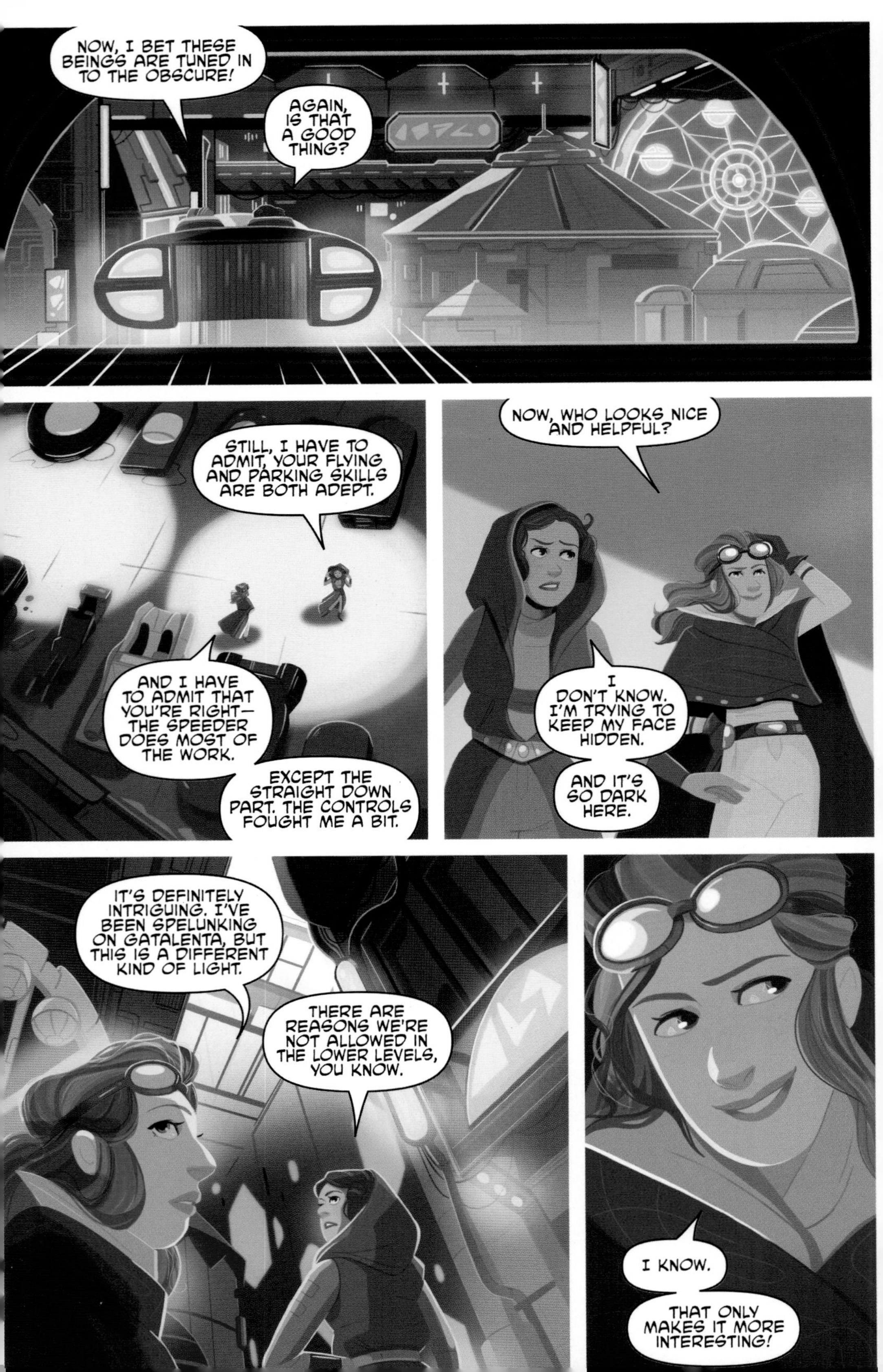
NOW, I BET THESE BEINGS ARE TUNED IN TO THE OBSCURE!
AGAIN, IS THAT A GOOD THING?
STILL, I HAVE TO ADMIT, YOUR FLYING AND PARKING SKILLS ARE BOTH ADEPT.
AND I HAVE TO ADMIT THAT YOU'RE RIGHT— THE SPEEDER DOES MOST OF THE WORK.
EXCEPT THE STRAIGHT DOWN PART. THE CONTROLS FOUGHT ME A BIT.
NOW, WHO LOOKS NICE AND HELPFUL?
I DON'T KNOW. I'M TRYING TO KEEP MY FACE HIDDEN.
AND IT'S SO DARK HERE.
IT'S DEFINITELY INTRIGUING. I'VE BEEN SPELUNKING ON GATALENTA, BUT THIS IS A DIFFERENT KIND OF LIGHT.
THERE ARE REASONS WE'RE NOT ALLOWED IN THE LOWER LEVELS, YOU KNOW.
I KNOW.
THAT ONLY MAKES IT MORE INTERESTING!

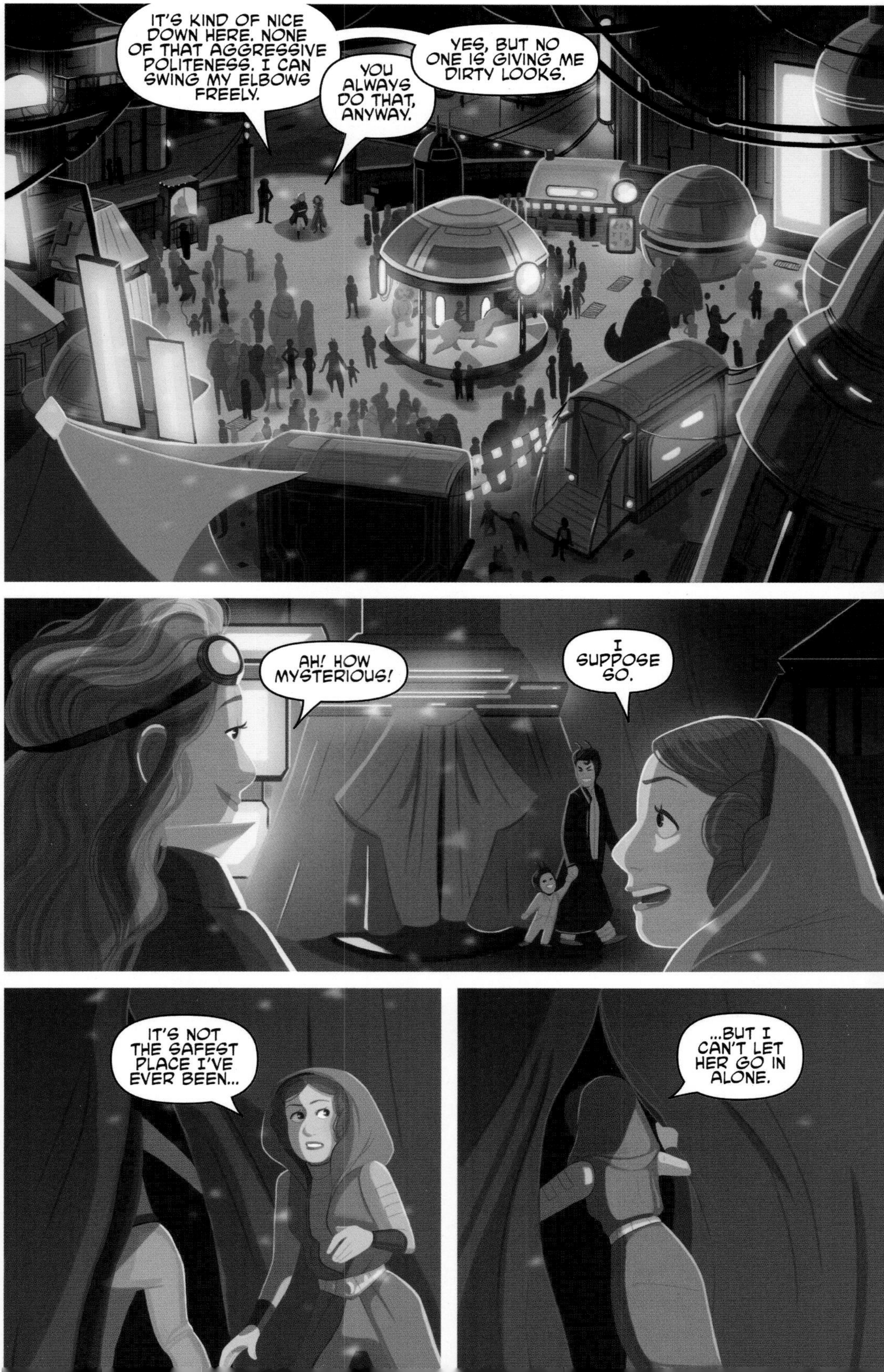
IT'S KIND OF NICE DOWN HERE. NONE OF THAT AGGRESSIVE POLITENESS. I CAN SWING MY ELBOWS FREELY.
YOU ALWAYS DO THAT, ANYWAY.
YES, BUT NO ONE IS GIVING ME DIRTY LOOKS.
AH! HOW MYSTERIOUS!
I SUPPOSE SO.
IT'S NOT THE SAFEST PLACE I'VE EVER BEEN...
...BUT I CAN'T LET HER GO IN ALONE.

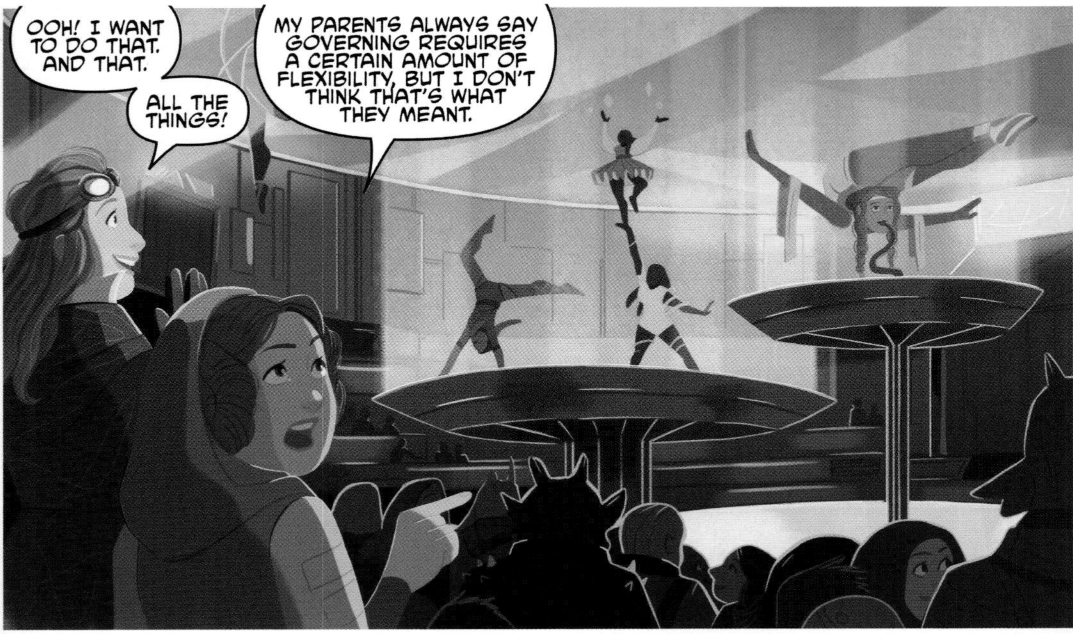
OOH! I WANT TO DO THAT. AND THAT.
ALL THE THINGS!
MY PARENTS ALWAYS SAY GOVERNING REQUIRES A CERTAIN AMOUNT OF FLEXIBILITY, BUT I DON'T THINK THAT'S WHAT THEY MEANT.

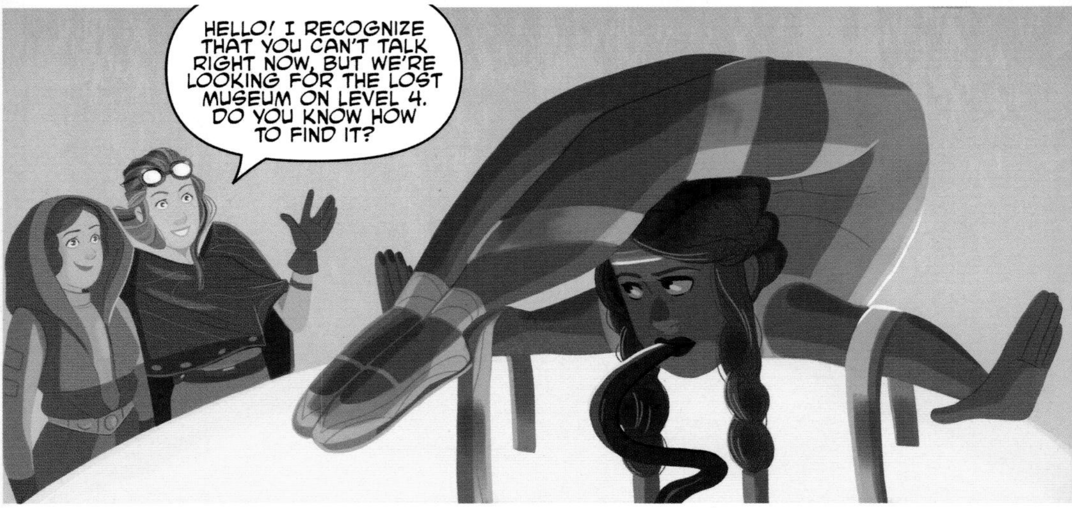
HELLO! I RECOGNIZE THAT YOU CAN'T TALK RIGHT NOW, BUT WE'RE LOOKING FOR THE LOST MUSEUM ON LEVEL 4. DO YOU KNOW HOW TO FIND IT?

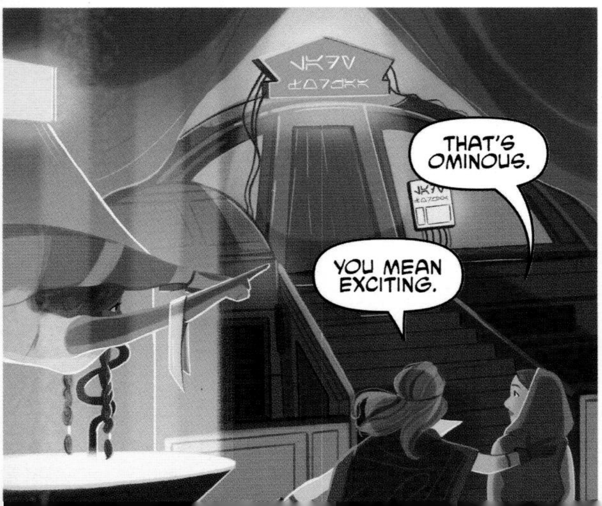
THAT'S OMINOUS.
YOU MEAN EXCITING.

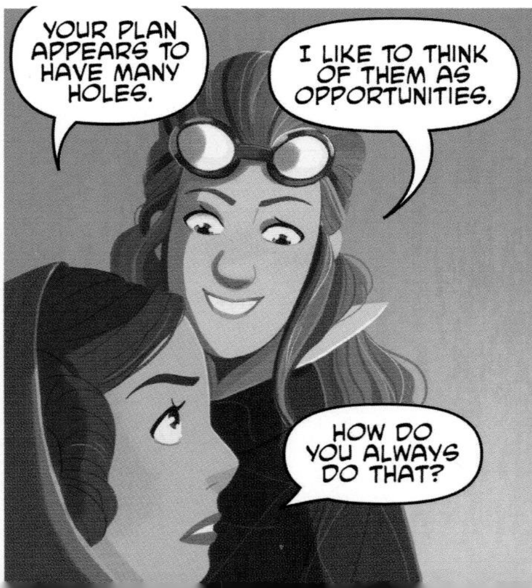
YOUR PLAN APPEARS TO HAVE MANY HOLES.
I LIKE TO THINK OF THEM AS OPPORTUNITIES.
HOW DO YOU ALWAYS DO THAT?

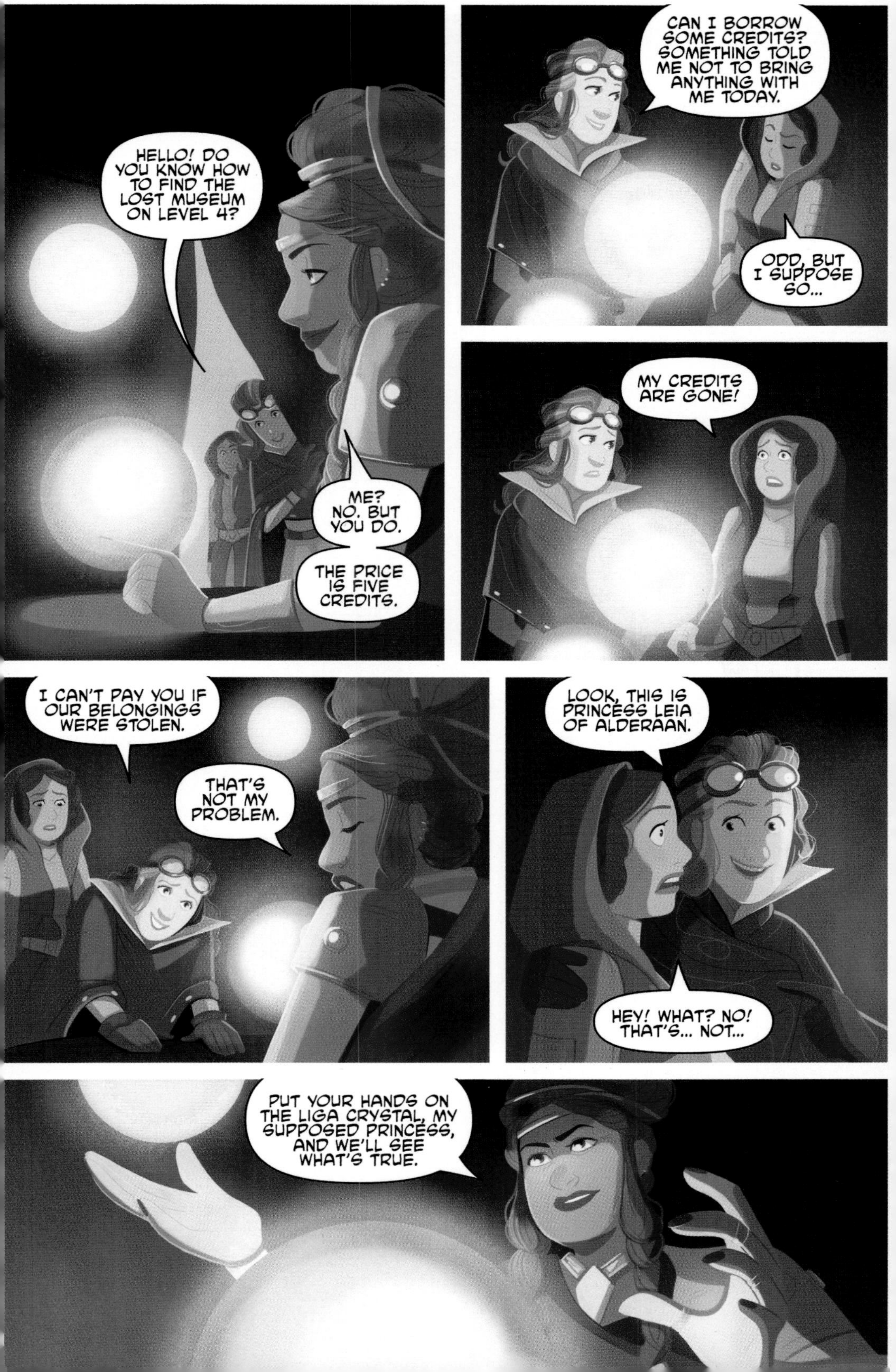
HELLO! DO YOU KNOW HOW TO FIND THE LOST MUSEUM ON LEVEL 4?
ME? NO. BUT YOU DO.
THE PRICE IS FIVE CREDITS.
CAN I BORROW SOME CREDITS? SOMETHING TOLD ME NOT TO BRING ANYTHING WITH ME TODAY.
ODD, BUT I SUPPOSE SO...
MY CREDITS ARE GONE!
I CAN'T PAY YOU IF OUR BELONGINGS WERE STOLEN.
THAT'S NOT MY PROBLEM.
LOOK, THIS IS PRINCESS LEIA OF ALDERAAN.
HEY! WHAT? NO! THAT'S... NOT...
PUT YOUR HANDS ON THE LIGA CRYSTAL, MY SUPPOSED PRINCESS, AND WE'LL SEE WHAT'S TRUE.

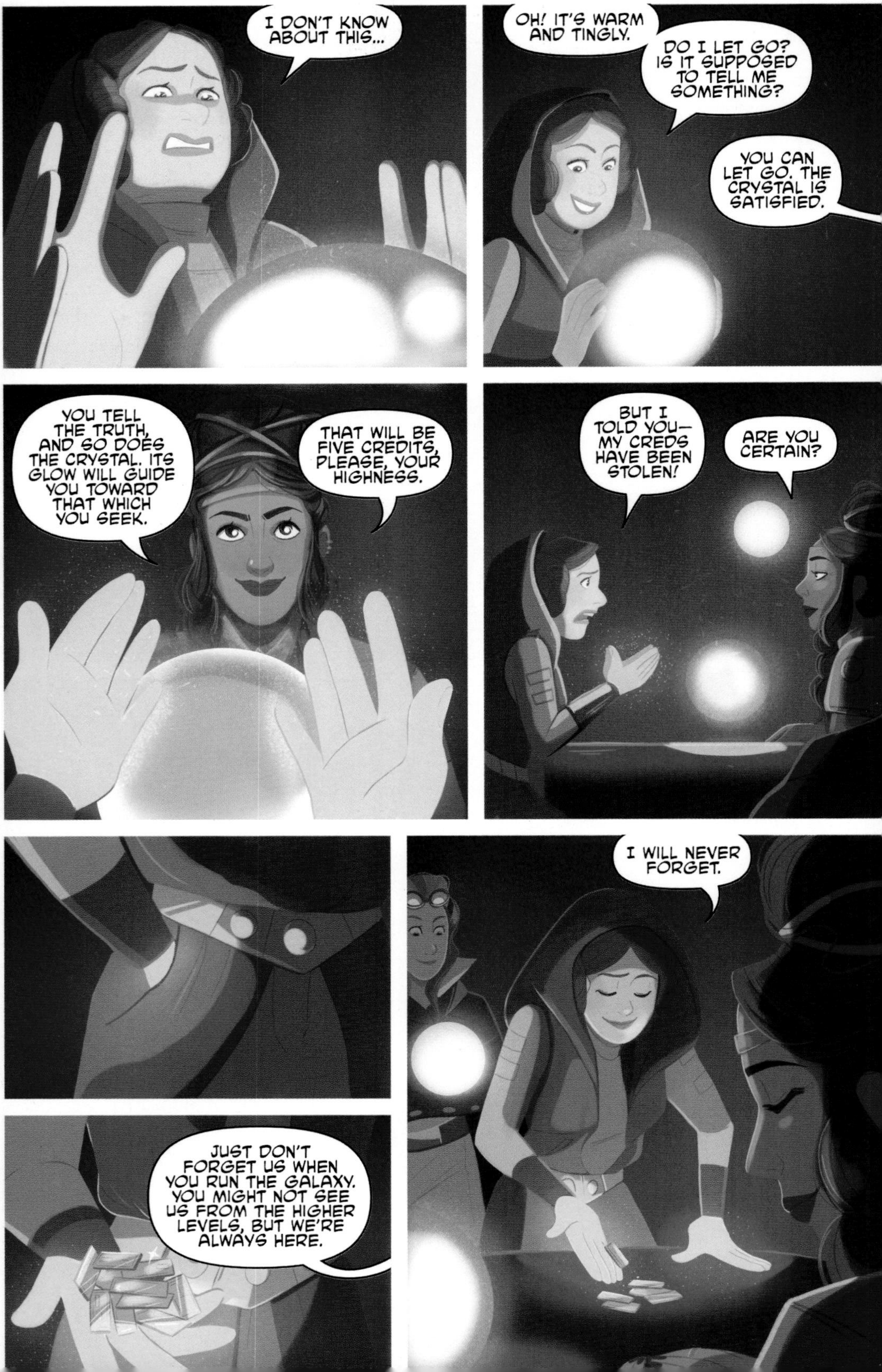
I DON'T KNOW ABOUT THIS...
OH! IT'S WARM AND TINGLY.
DO I LET GO? IS IT SUPPOSED TO TELL ME SOMETHING?
YOU CAN LET GO. THE CRYSTAL IS SATISFIED.
YOU TELL THE TRUTH, AND SO DOES THE CRYSTAL. ITS GLOW WILL GUIDE YOU TOWARD THAT WHICH YOU SEEK.
THAT WILL BE FIVE CREDITS, PLEASE, YOUR HIGHNESS.
BUT I TOLD YOU— MY CREDS HAVE BEEN STOLEN!
ARE YOU CERTAIN?
JUST DON'T FORGET US WHEN YOU RUN THE GALAXY. YOU MIGHT NOT SEE US FROM THE HIGHER LEVELS, BUT WE'RE ALWAYS HERE.
I WILL NEVER FORGET.

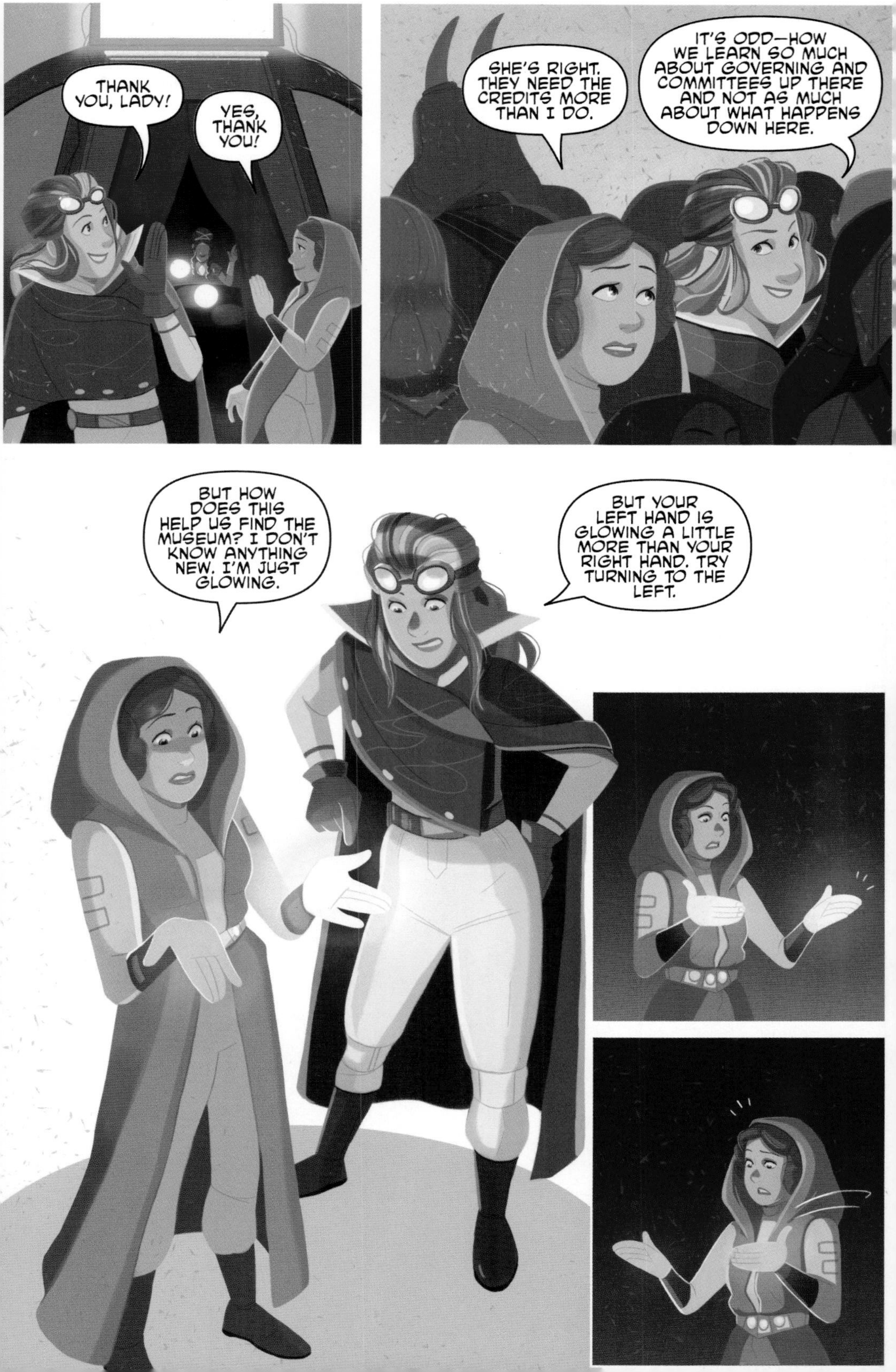
THANK YOU, LADY!
YES, THANK YOU!
SHE'S RIGHT. THEY NEED THE CREDITS MORE THAN I DO.
IT'S ODD—HOW WE LEARN SO MUCH ABOUT GOVERNING AND COMMITTEES UP THERE AND NOT AS MUCH ABOUT WHAT HAPPENS DOWN HERE.
BUT HOW DOES THIS HELP US FIND THE MUSEUM? I DON'T KNOW ANYTHING NEW. I'M JUST GLOWING.
BUT YOUR LEFT HAND IS GLOWING A LITTLE MORE THAN YOUR RIGHT HAND. TRY TURNING TO THE LEFT.

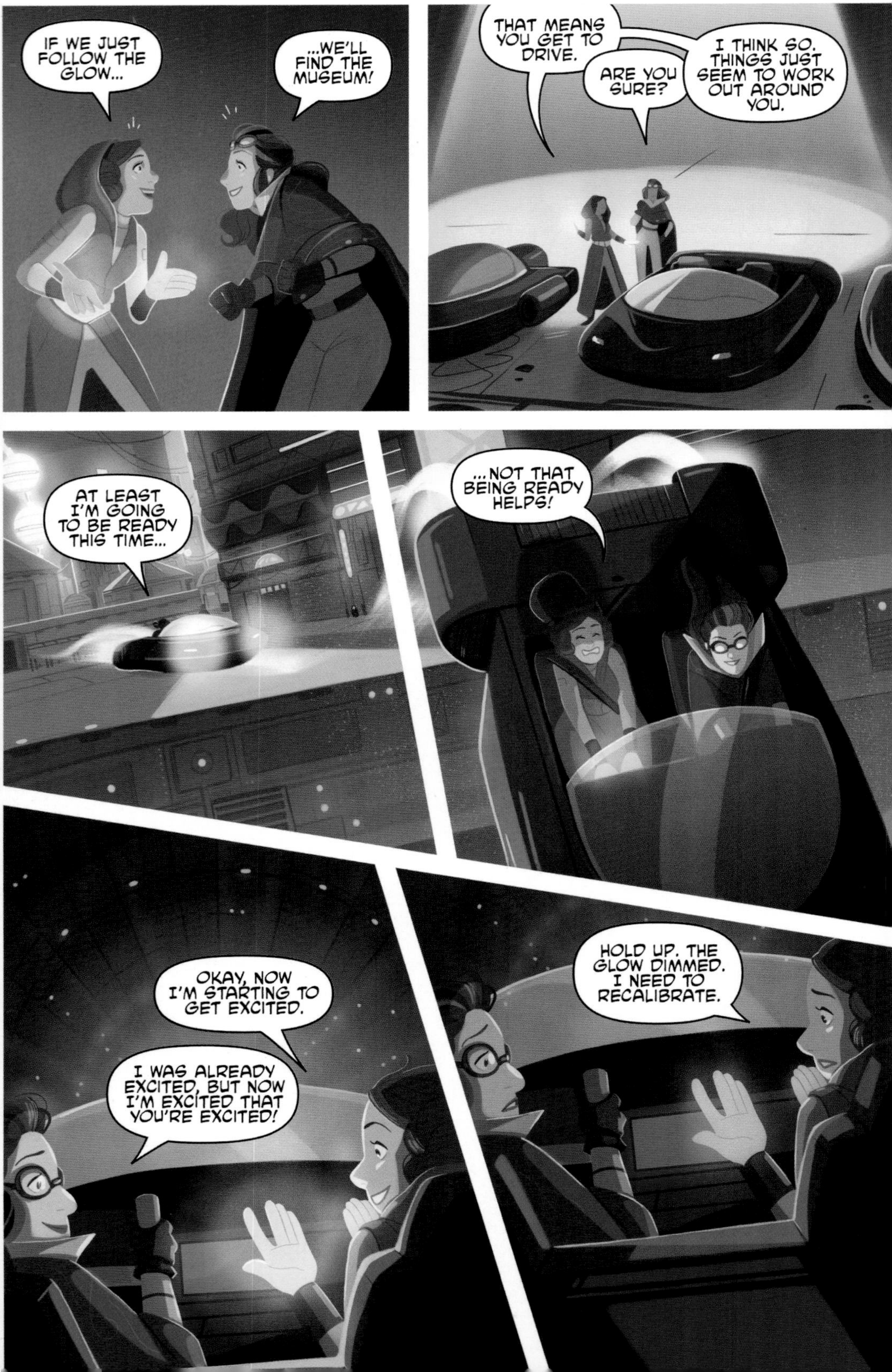
IF WE JUST FOLLOW THE GLOW...
...WE'LL FIND THE MUSEUM!
THAT MEANS YOU GET TO DRIVE.
ARE YOU SURE?
I THINK SO. THINGS JUST SEEM TO WORK OUT AROUND YOU.
AT LEAST I'M GOING TO BE READY THIS TIME...
...NOT THAT BEING READY HELPS!
OKAY, NOW I'M STARTING TO GET EXCITED.
I WAS ALREADY EXCITED, BUT NOW I'M EXCITED THAT YOU'RE EXCITED!
HOLD UP. THE GLOW DIMMED. I NEED TO RECALIBRATE.

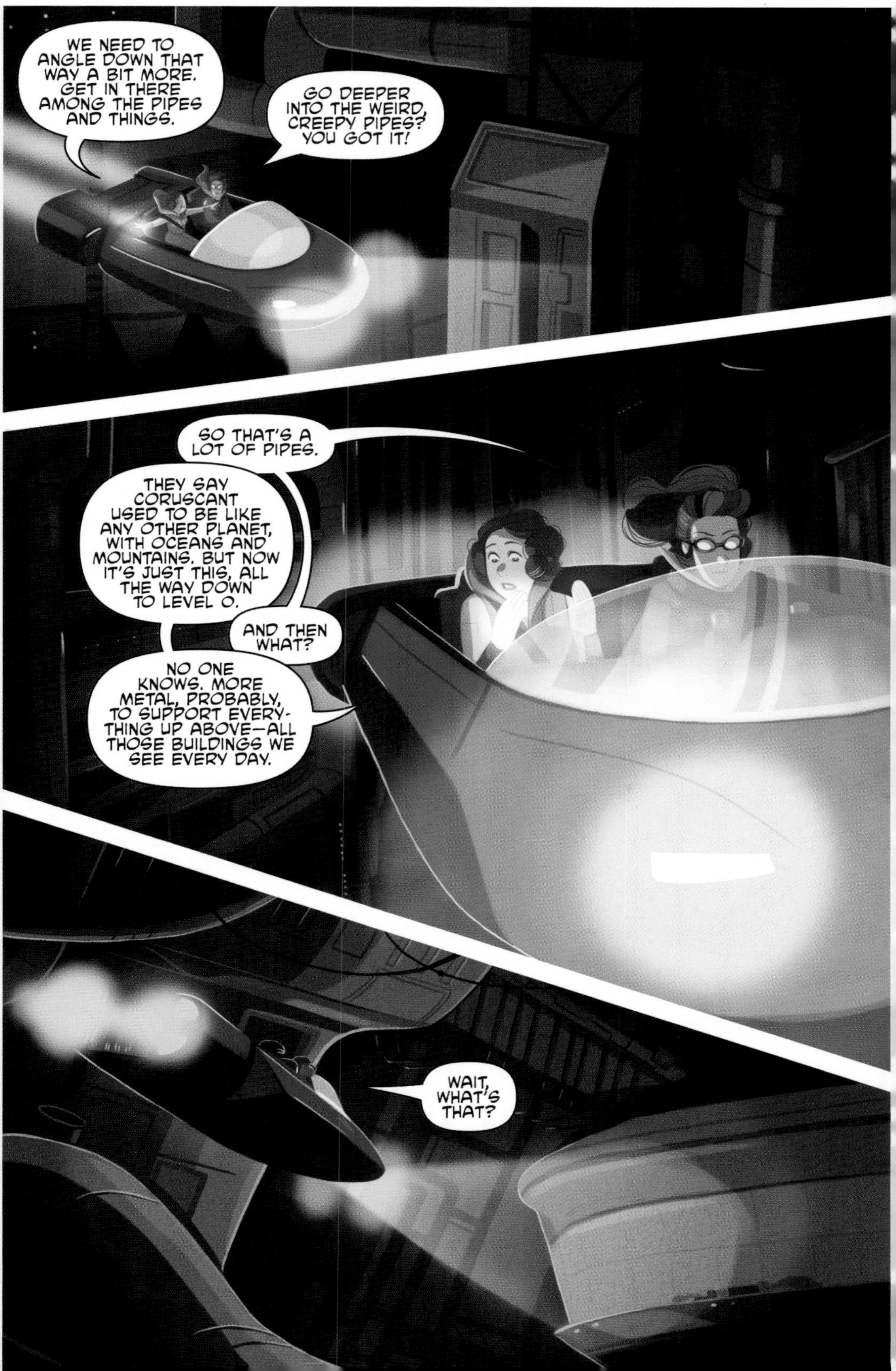
WE NEED TO ANGLE DOWN THAT WAY A BIT MORE. GET IN THERE AMONG THE PIPES AND THINGS.
GO DEEPER INTO THE WEIRD, CREEPY PIPES? YOU GOT IT!
SO THAT'S A LOT OF PIPES.
THEY SAY CORUSCANT USED TO BE LIKE ANY OTHER PLANET, WITH OCEANS AND MOUNTAINS. BUT NOW IT'S JUST THIS, ALL THE WAY DOWN TO LEVEL 0.
AND THEN WHAT?
NO ONE KNOWS. MORE METAL, PROBABLY, TO SUPPORT EVERY-THING UP ABOVE—ALL THOSE BUILDINGS WE SEE EVERY DAY.
WAIT, WHAT'S THAT?

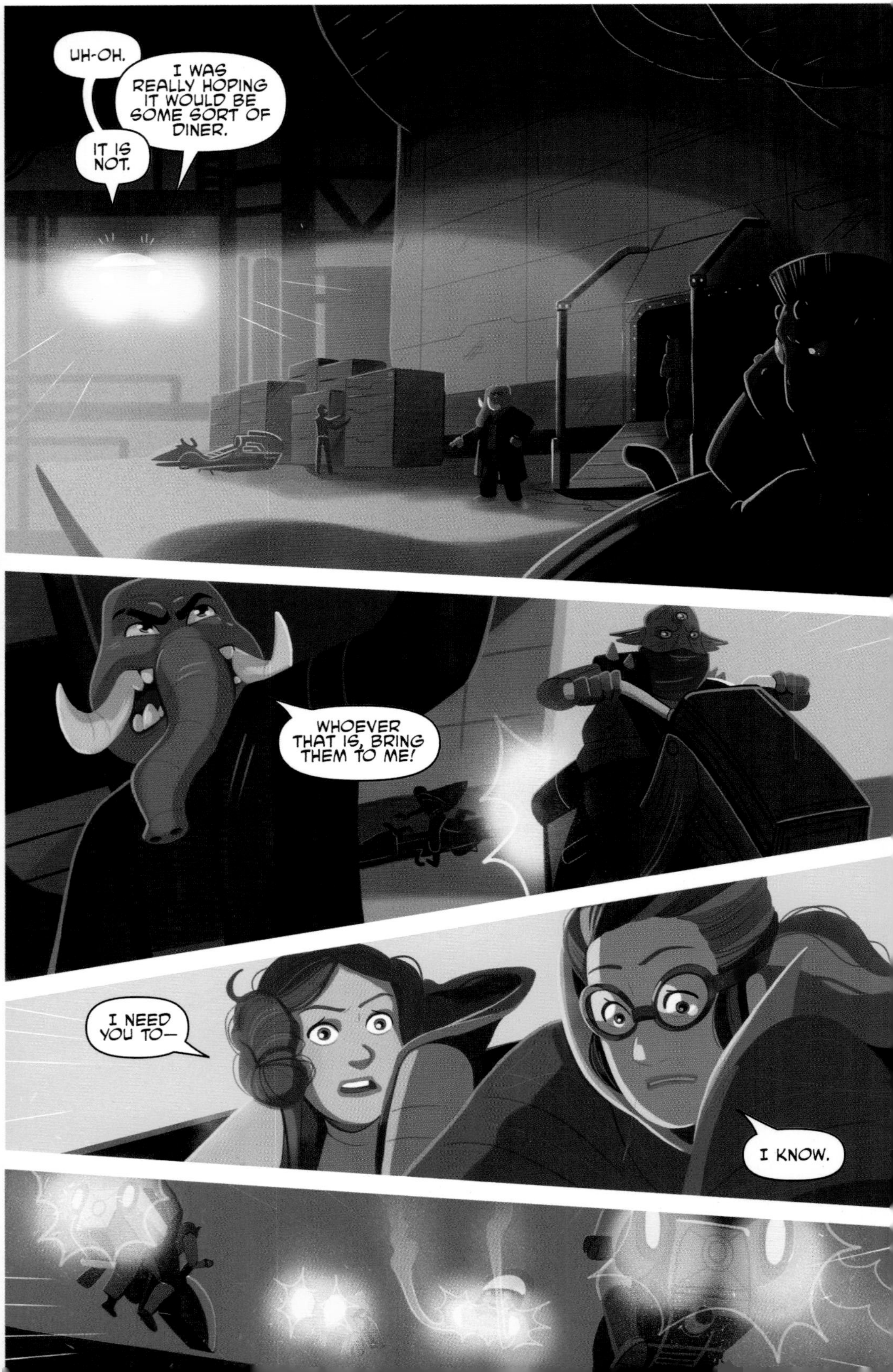
UH-OH.
I WAS REALLY HOPING IT WOULD BE SOME SORT OF DINER.
IT IS NOT.
WHOEVER THAT IS, BRING THEM TO ME!
I NEED YOU TO—
I KNOW.

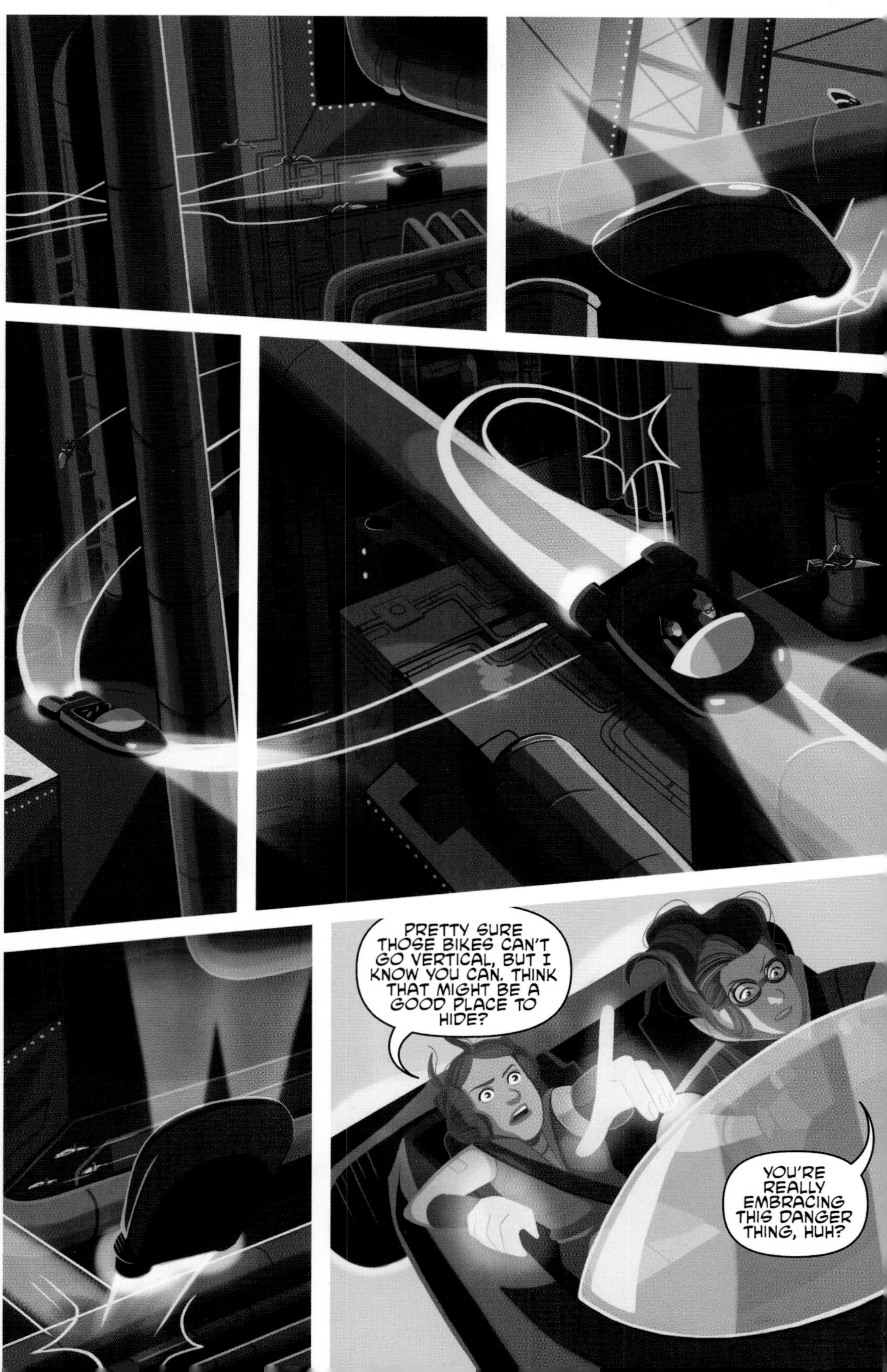
PRETTY SURE THOSE BIKES CAN'T GO VERTICAL, BUT I KNOW YOU CAN. THINK THAT MIGHT BE A GOOD PLACE TO HIDE?
YOU'RE REALLY EMBRACING THIS DANGER THING, HUH?

NOW IS NOT THE BEST TIME TO HAVE GLOWING HANDS.

THANK GOODNESS FOR POCKETS!

I THOUGHT WE HAD 'EM.

BOSS IS GONNA BE MAD.

SO LET'S TOSS A THERMAL DETONATOR AGAINST A PIPE AND SAY THEY RAN INTO SOMETHING AND BLEW UP.

AGAIN? HE'S GONNA CATCH ON ONE DAY.

HOPEFULLY NOT TODAY.

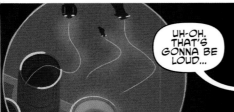

UH-OH, THAT'S GONNA BE LOUD...

KRAKOOM

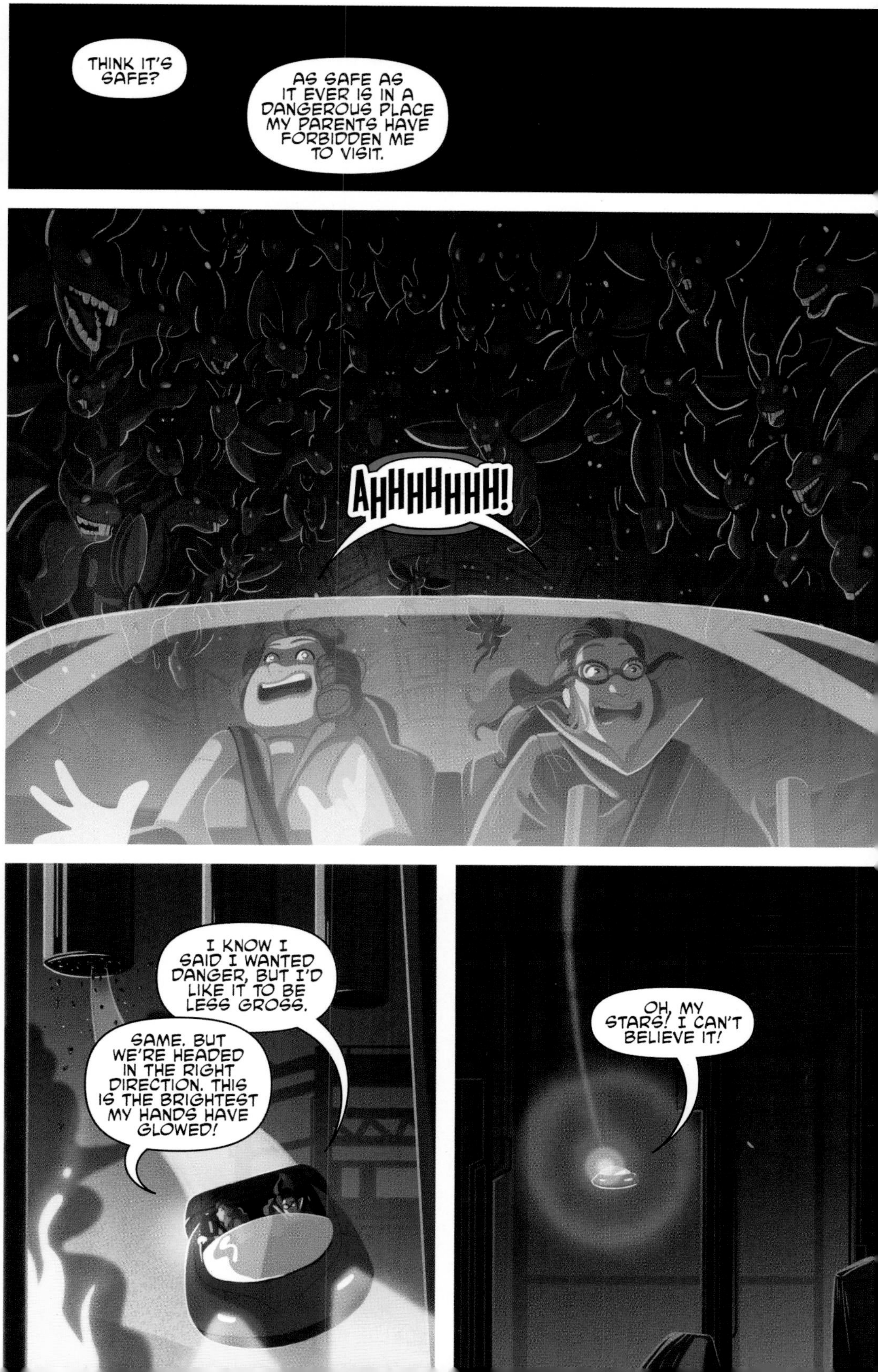
THINK IT'S SAFE?
AS SAFE AS IT EVER IS IN A DANGEROUS PLACE MY PARENTS HAVE FORBIDDEN ME TO VISIT.
AHHHHHHH!
I KNOW I SAID I WANTED DANGER, BUT I'D LIKE IT TO BE LESS GROSS.
SAME. BUT WE'RE HEADED IN THE RIGHT DIRECTION. THIS IS THE BRIGHTEST MY HANDS HAVE GLOWED!
OH, MY STARS! I CAN'T BELIEVE IT!

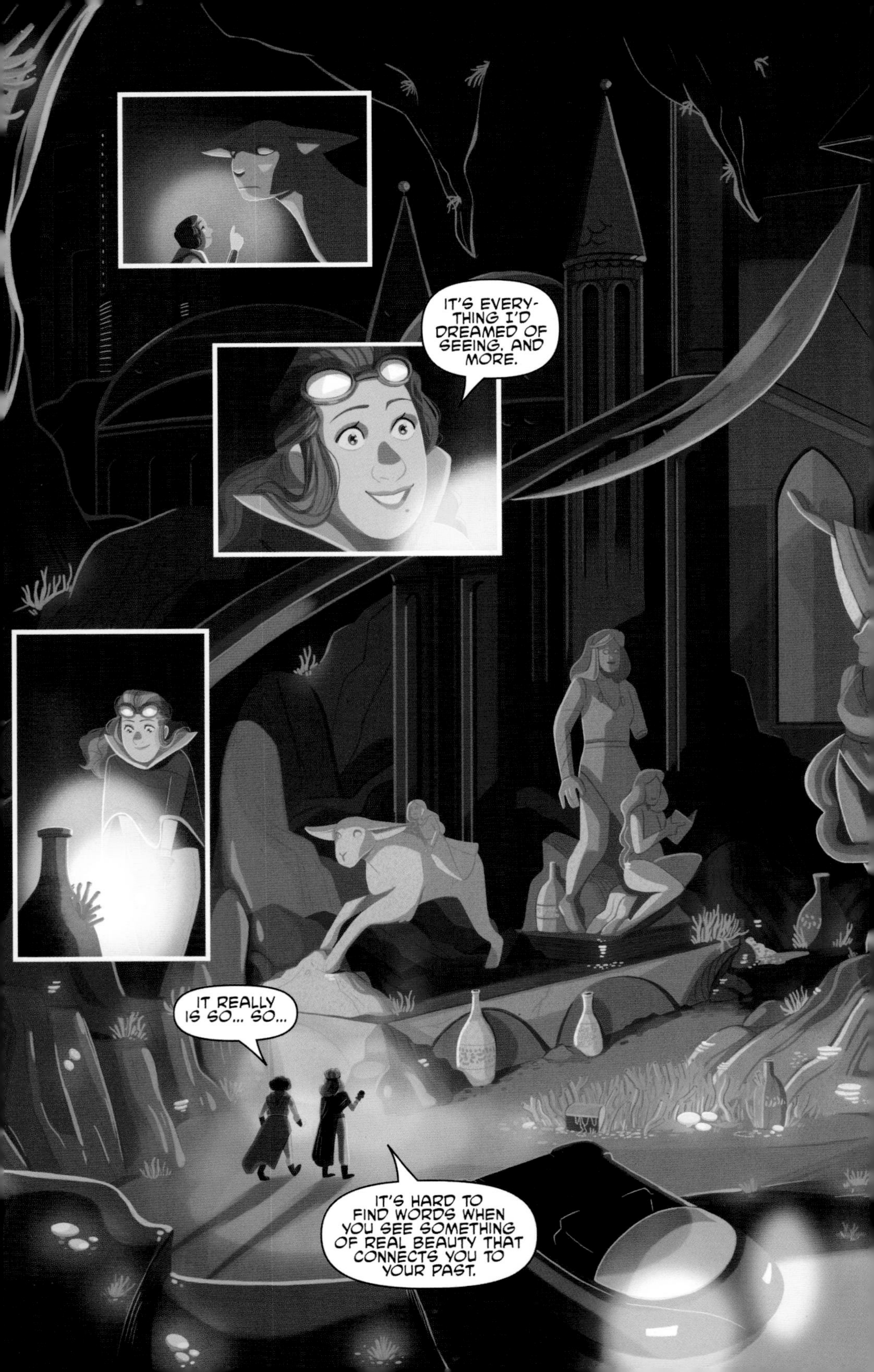
IT'S EVERY-
THING I'D
DREAMED OF
SEEING, AND
MORE.
IT REALLY
IS SO... SO...
IT'S HARD TO
FIND WORDS WHEN
YOU SEE SOMETHING
OF REAL BEAUTY THAT
CONNECTS YOU TO
YOUR PAST.

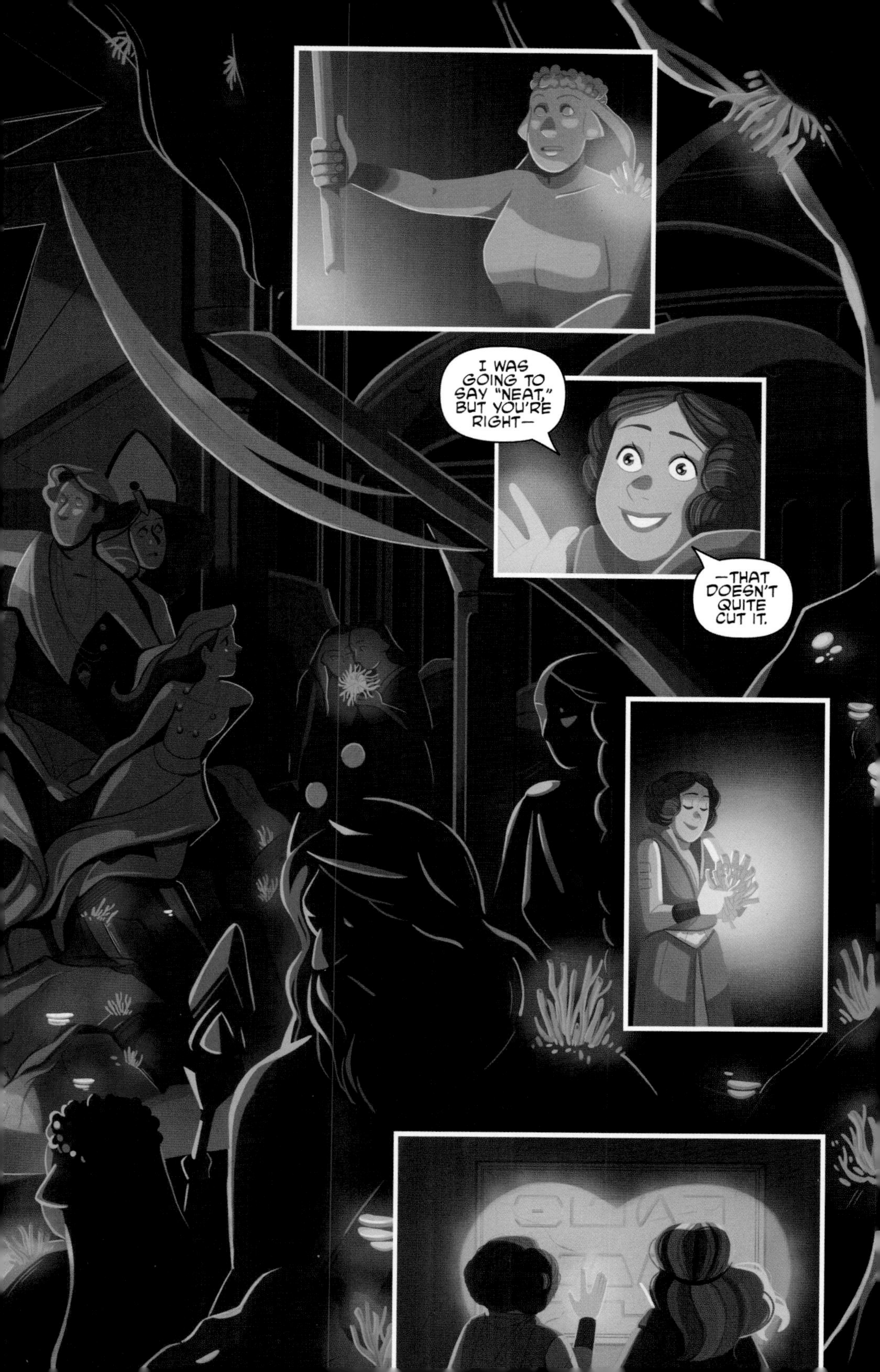
I WAS GOING TO SAY "NEAT," BUT YOU'RE RIGHT—
—THAT DOESN'T QUITE CUT IT.

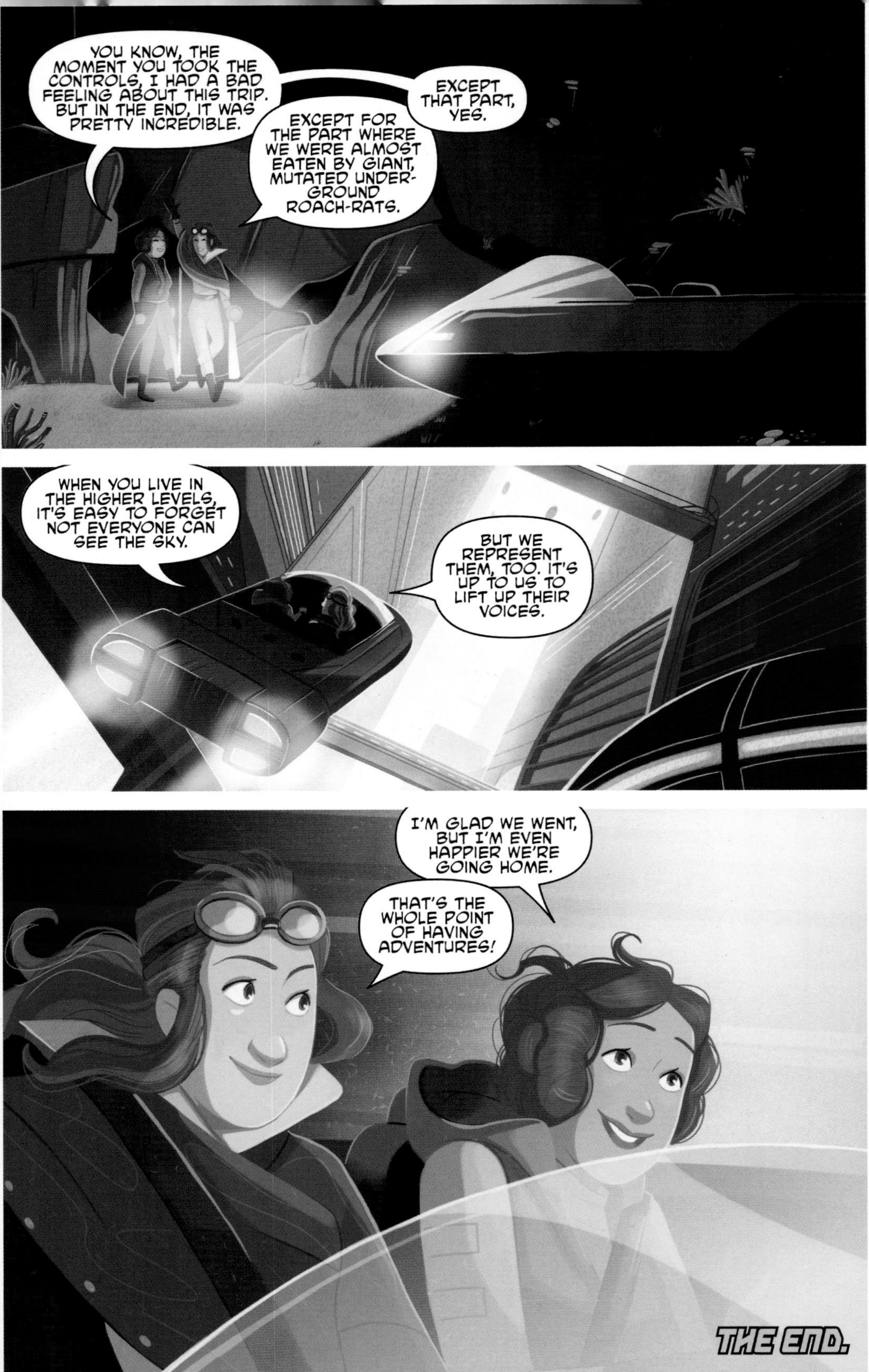
YOU KNOW, THE MOMENT YOU TOOK THE CONTROLS, I HAD A BAD FEELING ABOUT THIS TRIP. BUT IN THE END, IT WAS PRETTY INCREDIBLE.
EXCEPT FOR THE PART WHERE WE WERE ALMOST EATEN BY GIANT, MUTATED UNDER-GROUND ROACH-RATS.
EXCEPT THAT PART, YES.
WHEN YOU LIVE IN THE HIGHER LEVELS, IT'S EASY TO FORGET NOT EVERYONE CAN SEE THE SKY.
BUT WE REPRESENT THEM, TOO. IT'S UP TO US TO LIFT UP THEIR VOICES.
I'M GLAD WE WENT, BUT I'M EVEN HAPPIER WE'RE GOING HOME.
THAT'S THE WHOLE POINT OF HAVING ADVENTURES!
THE END.

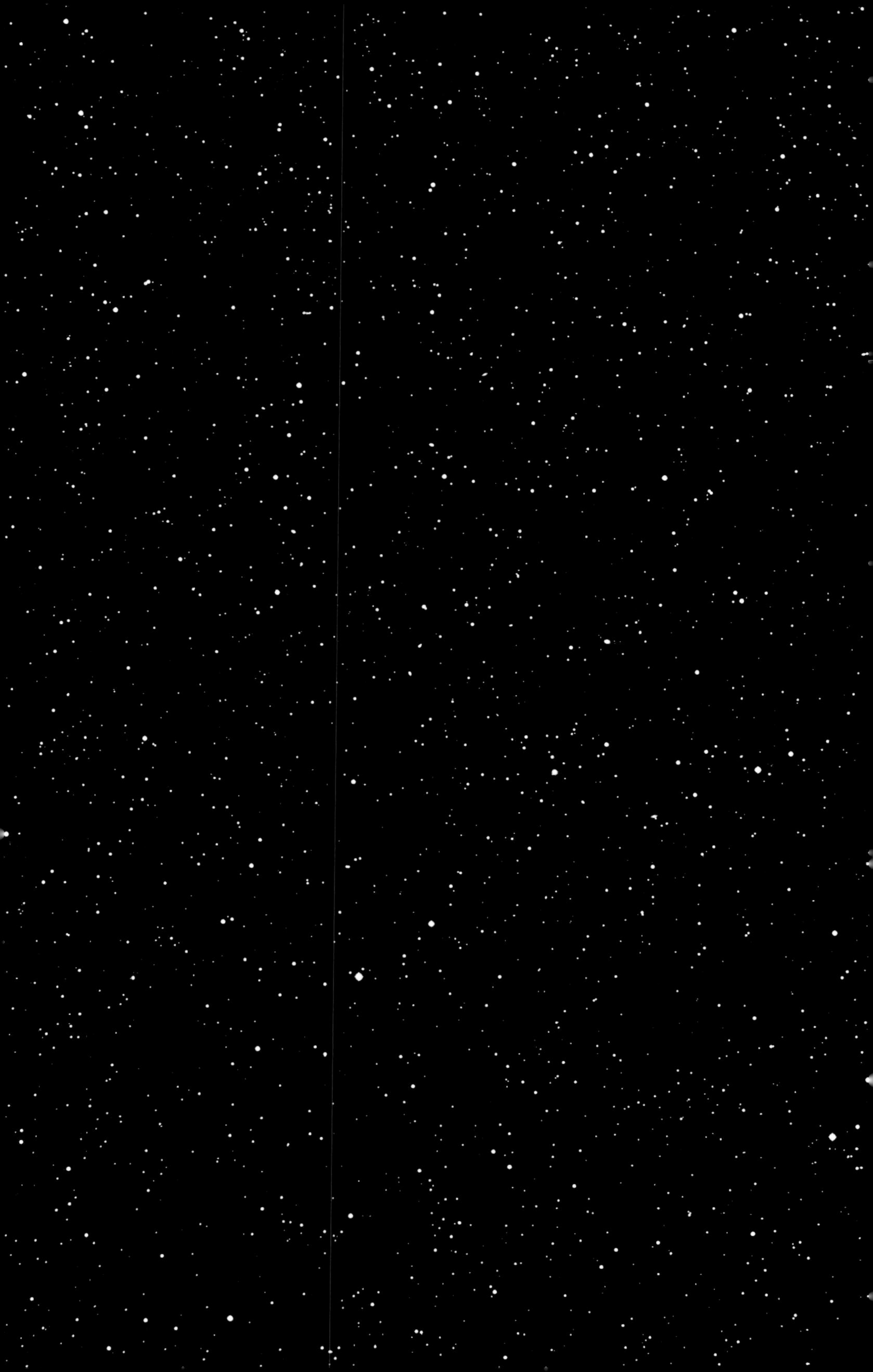

STAR WARS
ADVENTURES

Life Lessons

WRITER
CAVAN SCOTT

ARTIST
DEREK CHARM

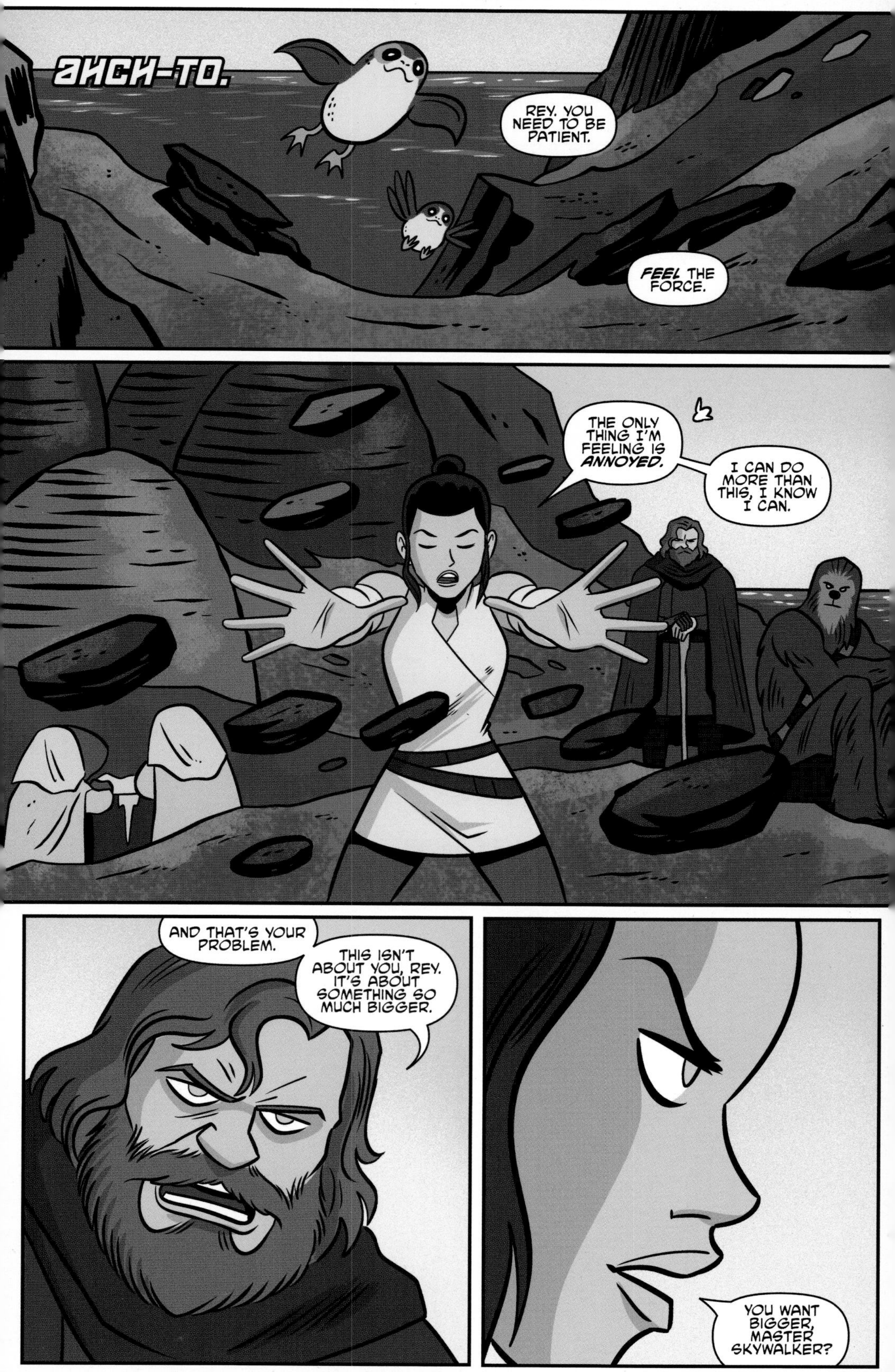
AHCH-TO.
REY. YOU NEED TO BE PATIENT.
FEEL THE FORCE.
THE ONLY THING I'M FEELING IS ANNOYED.
I CAN DO MORE THAN THIS, I KNOW I CAN.
AND THAT'S YOUR PROBLEM.
THIS ISN'T ABOUT YOU, REY. IT'S ABOUT SOMETHING SO MUCH BIGGER.
YOU WANT BIGGER, MASTER SKYWALKER?

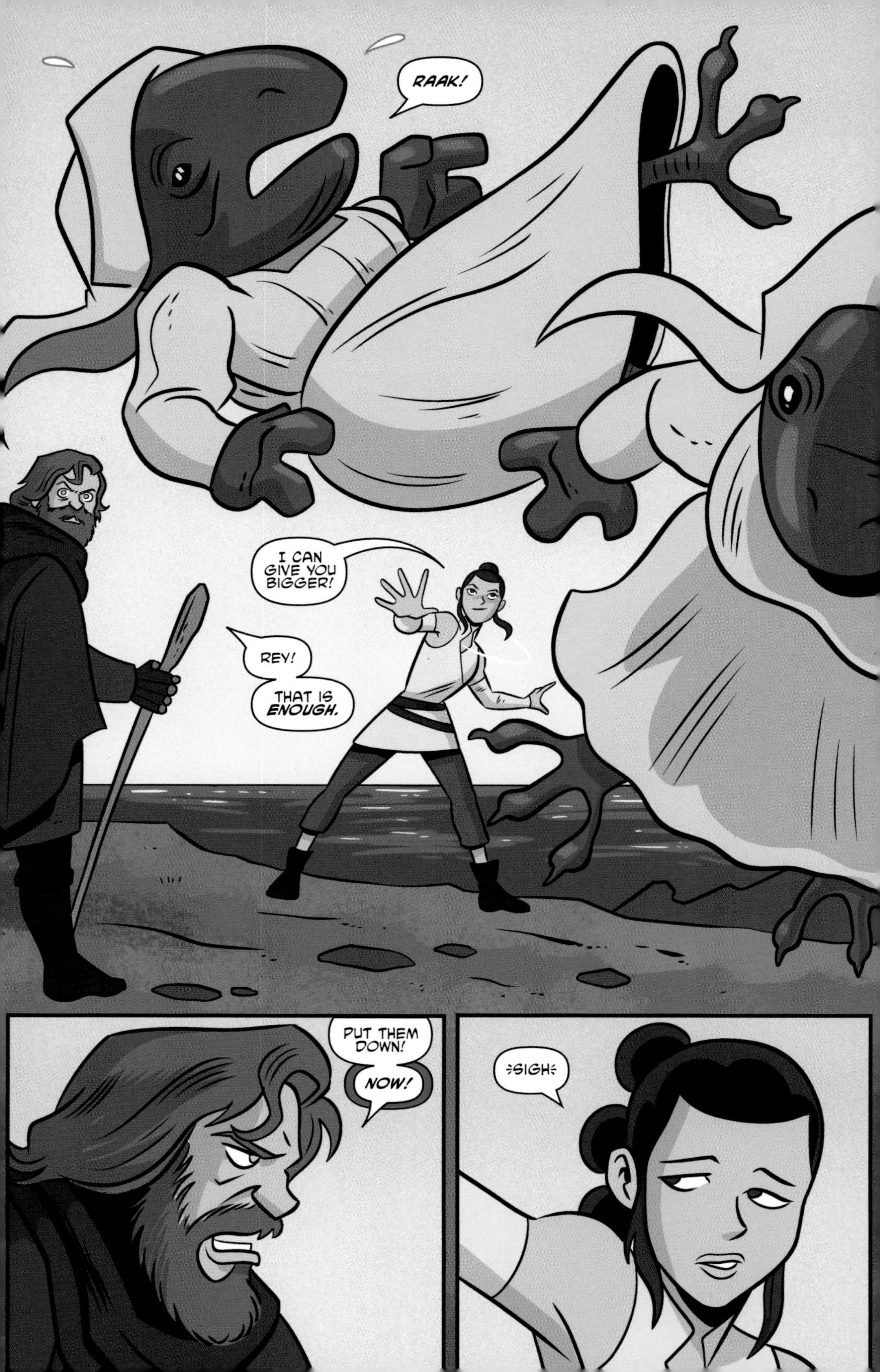
RAAK!
I CAN GIVE YOU BIGGER!
REY!
THAT IS *ENOUGH.*
PUT THEM DOWN!
NOW!
SIGH

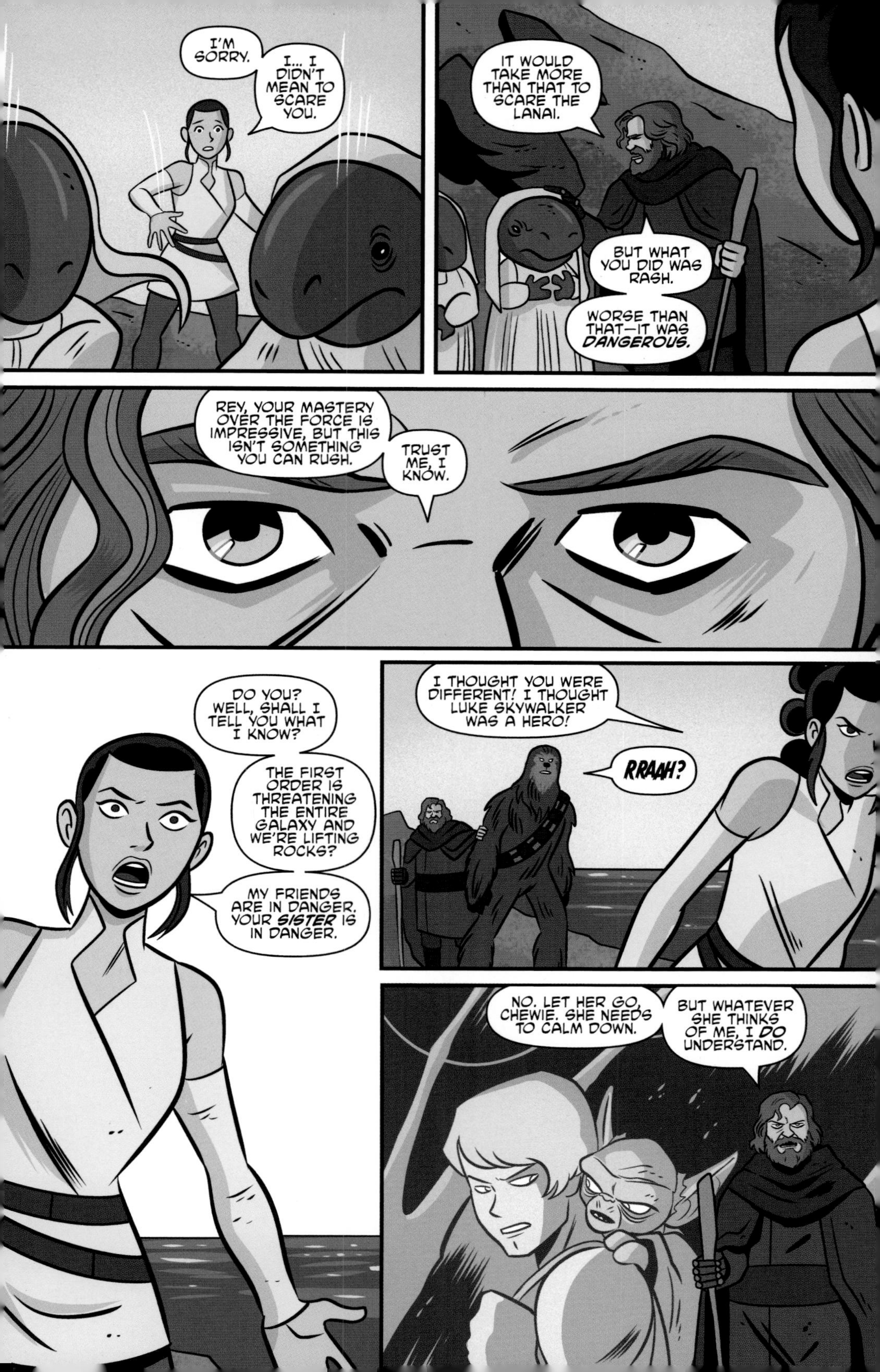
I'M SORRY.
I... I DIDN'T MEAN TO SCARE YOU.
IT WOULD TAKE MORE THAN THAT TO SCARE THE LANAI.
BUT WHAT YOU DID WAS RASH.
WORSE THAN THAT—IT WAS *DANGEROUS.*
REY, YOUR MASTERY OVER THE FORCE IS IMPRESSIVE, BUT THIS ISN'T SOMETHING YOU CAN RUSH.
TRUST ME, I KNOW.
DO YOU? WELL, SHALL I TELL YOU WHAT I KNOW?
THE FIRST ORDER IS THREATENING THE ENTIRE GALAXY AND WE'RE LIFTING ROCKS?
MY FRIENDS ARE IN DANGER. YOUR *SISTER* IS IN DANGER.
I THOUGHT YOU WERE DIFFERENT! I THOUGHT LUKE SKYWALKER WAS A HERO!
RRAAH?
NO. LET HER GO, CHEWIE. SHE NEEDS TO CALM DOWN.
BUT WHATEVER SHE THINKS OF ME, I *DO* UNDERSTAND.

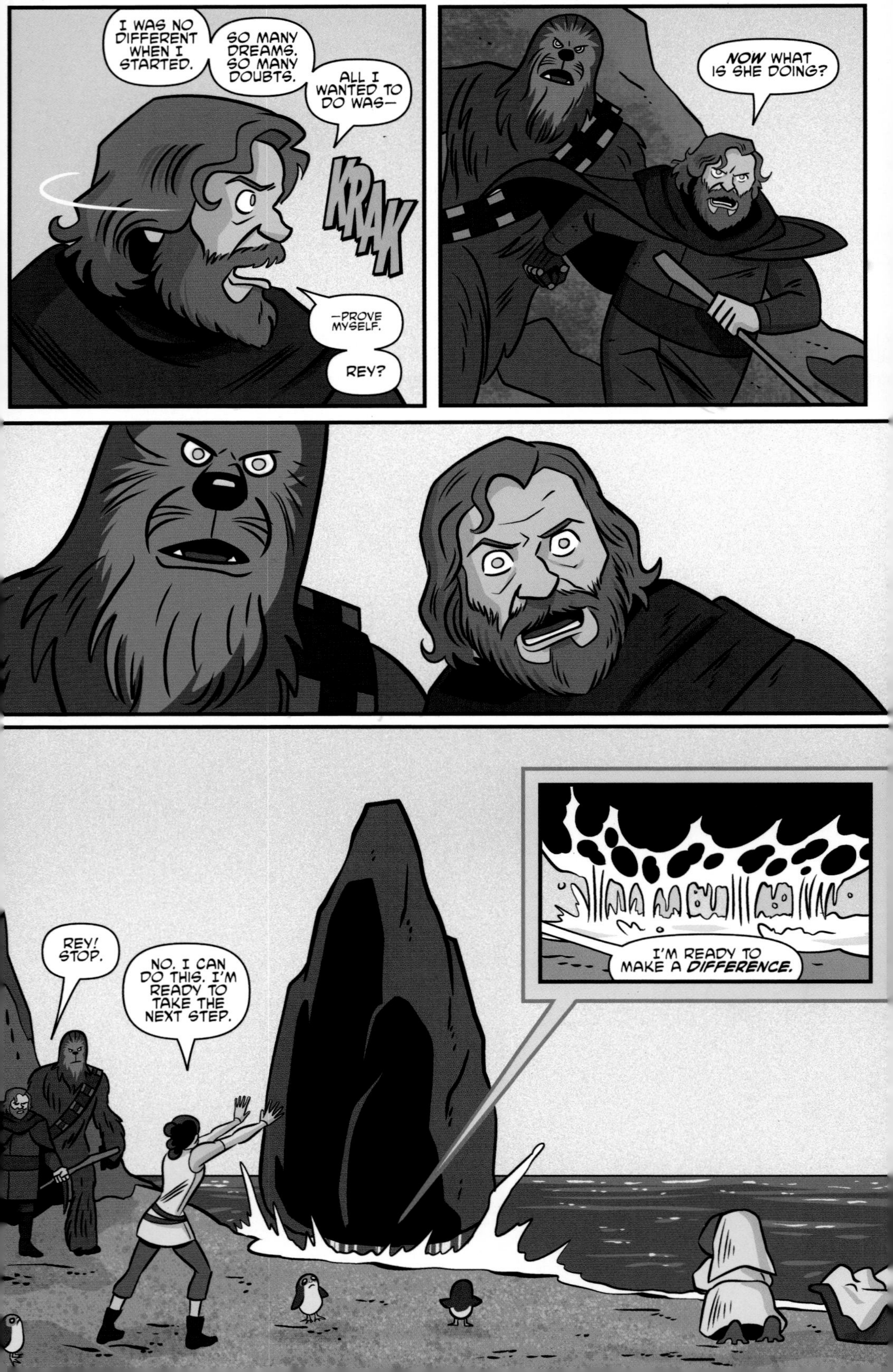

I WAS NO DIFFERENT WHEN I STARTED.
SO MANY DREAMS. SO MANY DOUBTS.
ALL I WANTED TO DO WAS—
KRAK
—PROVE MYSELF.
REY?
NOW WHAT IS SHE DOING?
REY! STOP.
NO. I CAN DO THIS. I'M READY TO TAKE THE NEXT STEP.
I'M READY TO MAKE A DIFFERENCE.

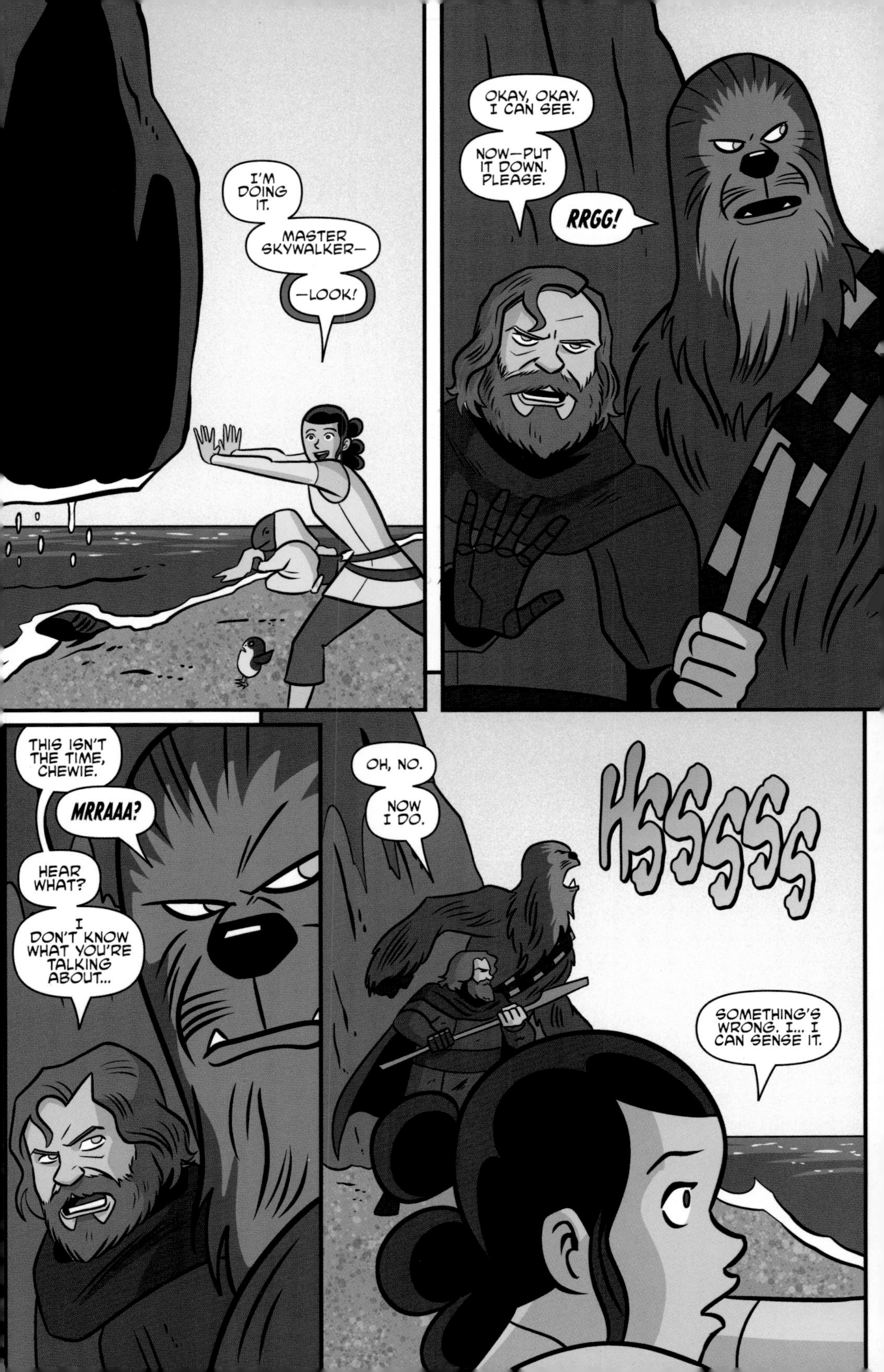
I'M DOING IT.
MASTER SKYWALKER—
—LOOK!
OKAY, OKAY. I CAN SEE.
NOW—PUT IT DOWN. PLEASE.
RRGG!
THIS ISN'T THE TIME, CHEWIE.
MRRAAA?
HEAR WHAT?
I DON'T KNOW WHAT YOU'RE TALKING ABOUT...
OH, NO.
NOW I DO.
HSSSSS
SOMETHING'S WRONG. I... I CAN SENSE IT.

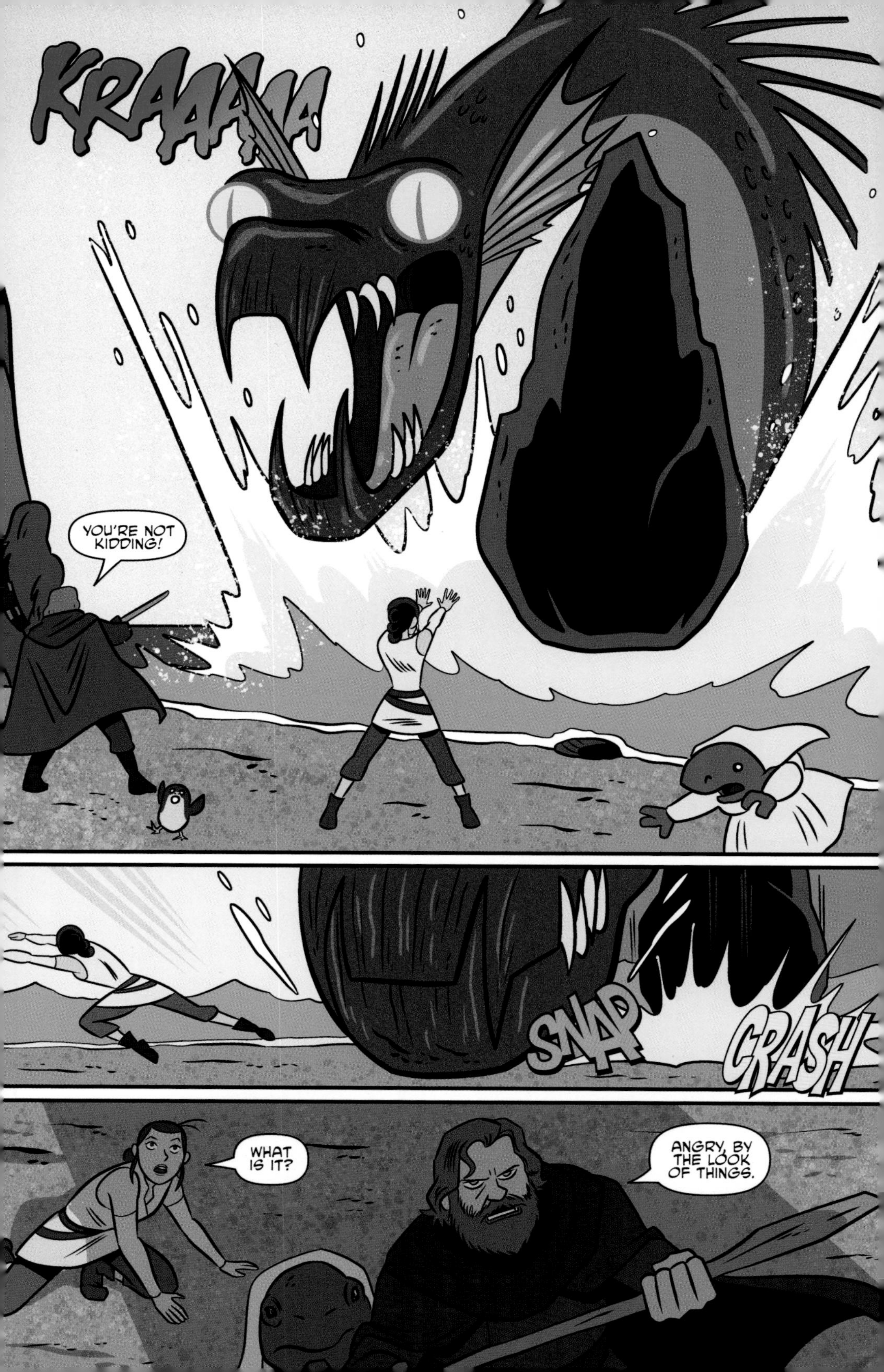
KRAAAAA
YOU'RE NOT KIDDING!
SNAP
CRASH
WHAT IS IT?
ANGRY, BY THE LOOK OF THINGS.

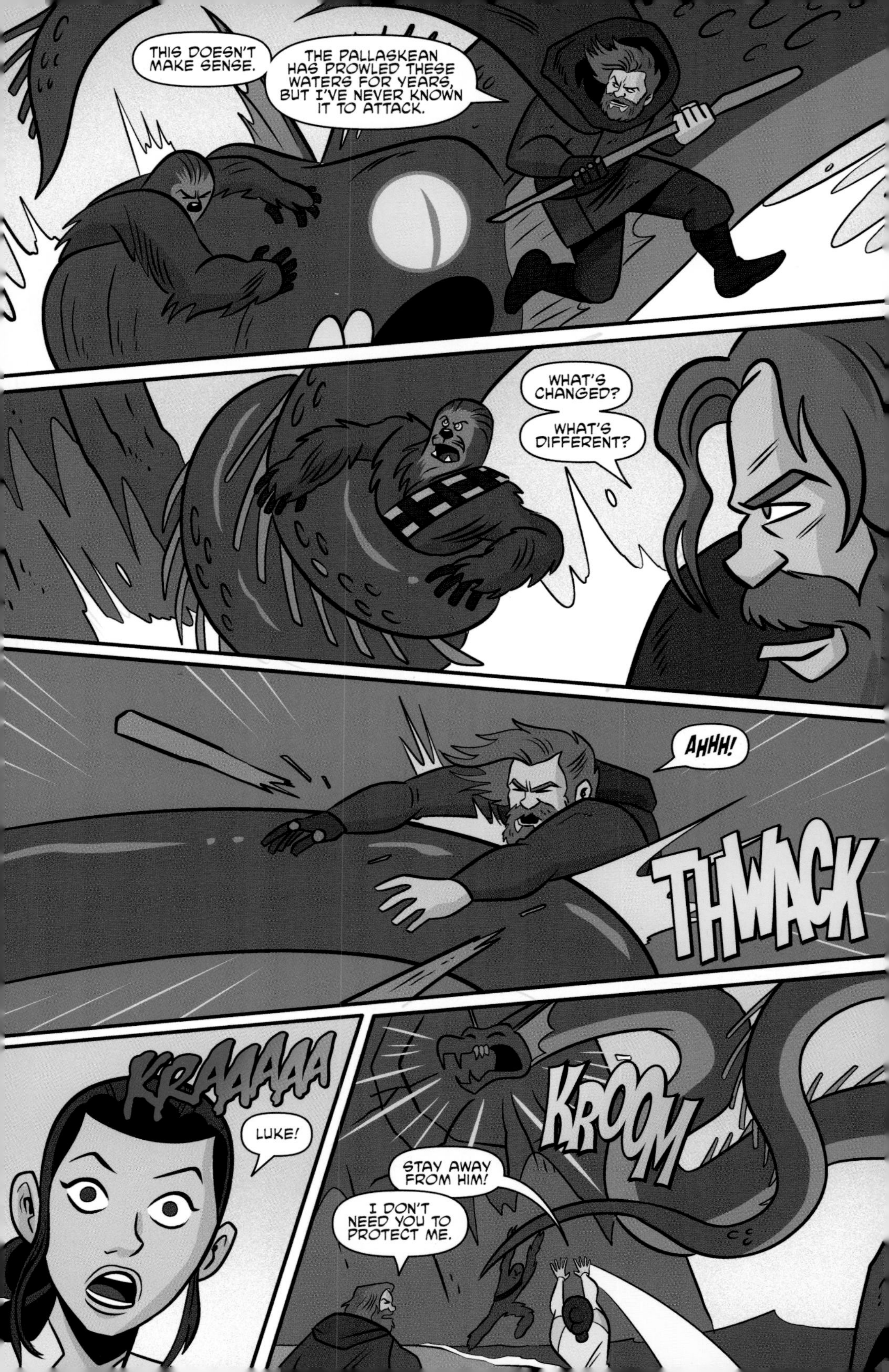
THIS DOESN'T MAKE SENSE.
THE PALLASKEAN HAS PROWLED THESE WATERS FOR YEARS, BUT I'VE NEVER KNOWN IT TO ATTACK.
WHAT'S CHANGED?
WHAT'S DIFFERENT?
AHHH!
THWACK
KRAAAAA
LUKE!
KROOM
STAY AWAY FROM HIM!
I DON'T NEED YOU TO PROTECT ME.

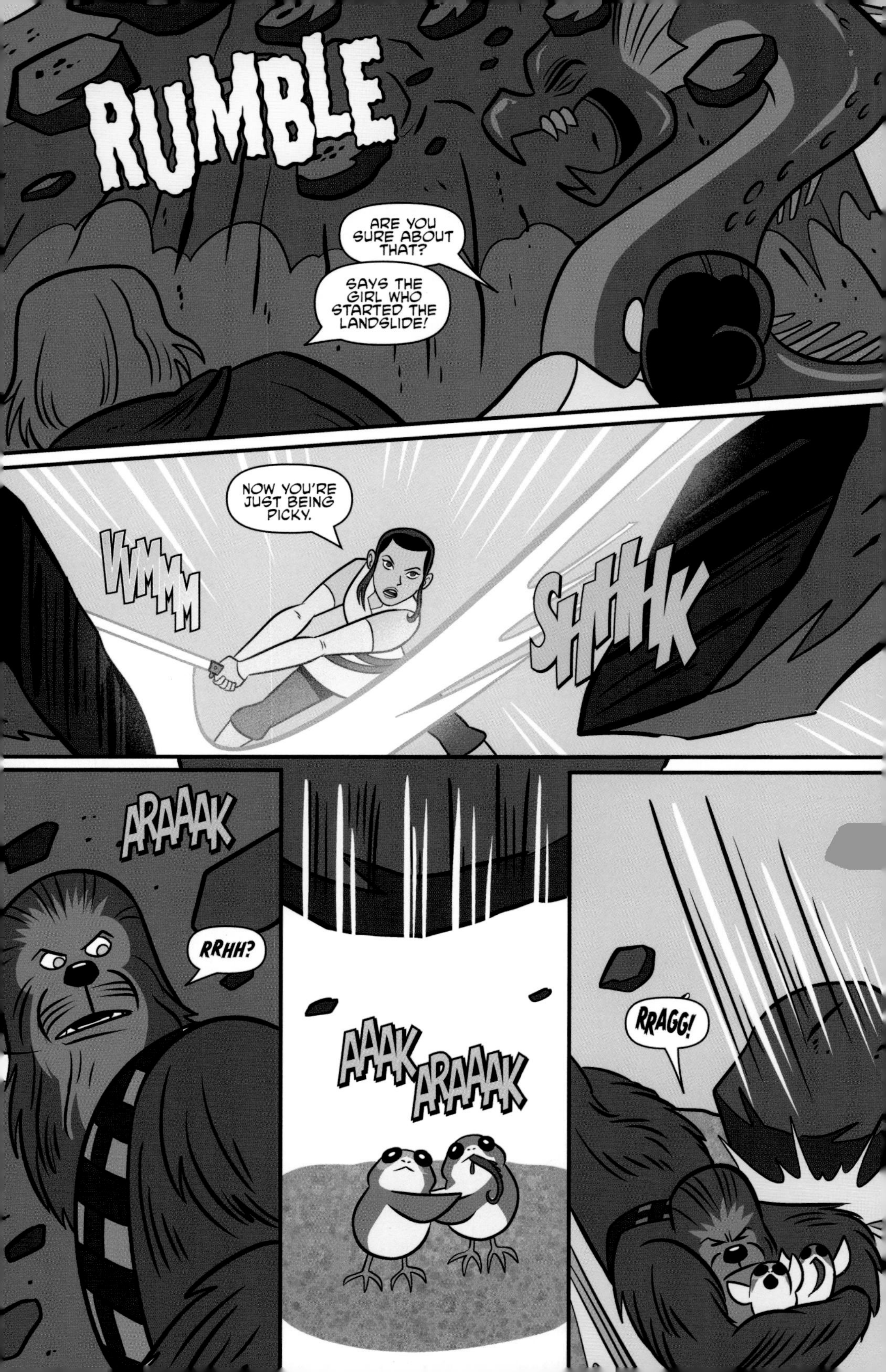
RUMBLE
ARE YOU SURE ABOUT THAT?
SAYS THE GIRL WHO STARTED THE LANDSLIDE!
NOW YOU'RE JUST BEING PICKY.
VVMMMM
SHHHK
ARAAAK
RRHH?
AAAK ARAAAK
RRAGG!

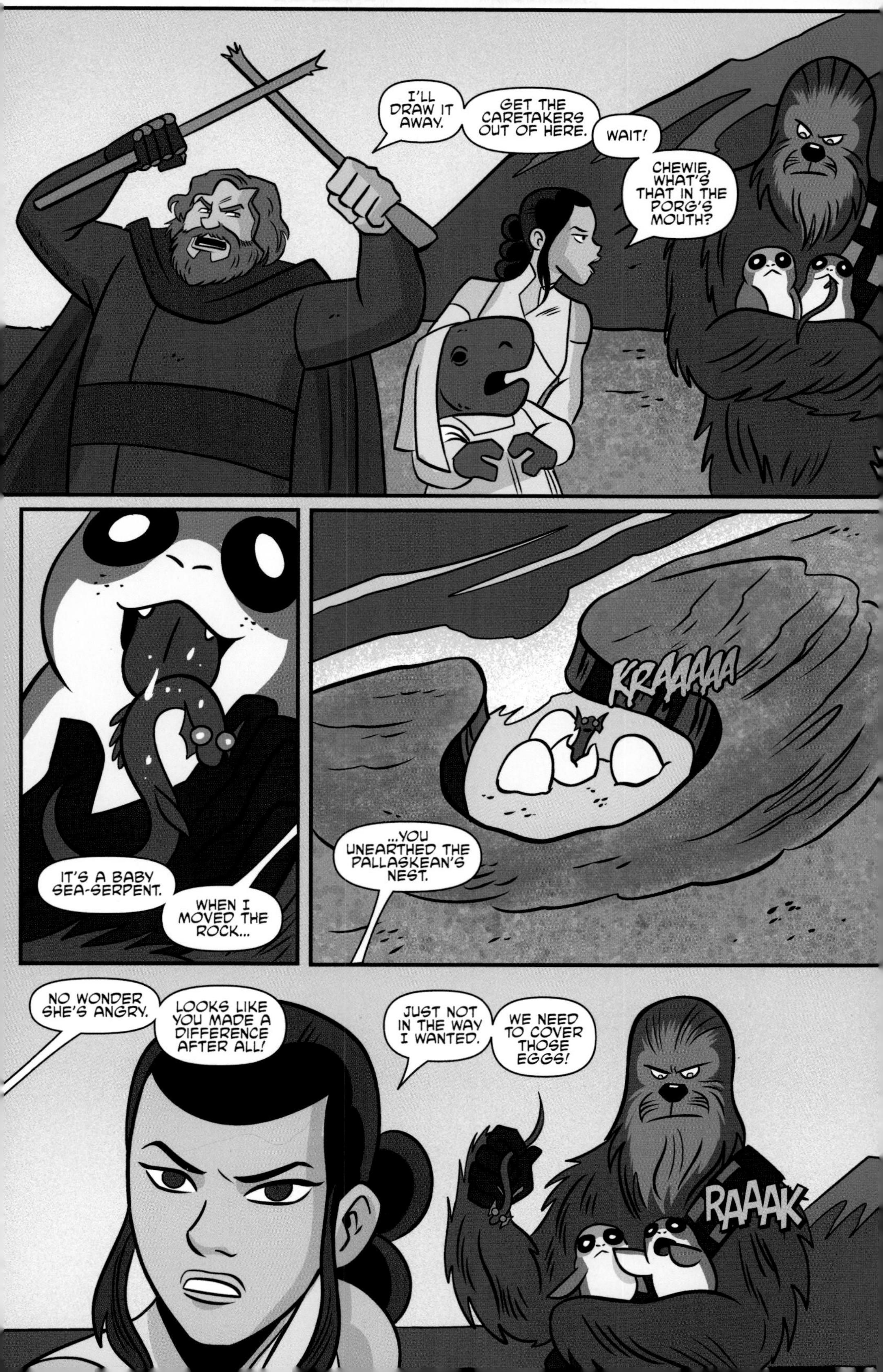
I'LL DRAW IT AWAY.
GET THE CARETAKERS OUT OF HERE.
WAIT!
CHEWIE, WHAT'S THAT IN THE PORG'S MOUTH?
IT'S A BABY SEA-SERPENT.
WHEN I MOVED THE ROCK...
...YOU UNEARTHED THE PALLASKEAN'S NEST.
KRAAAAA
NO WONDER SHE'S ANGRY.
LOOKS LIKE YOU MADE A DIFFERENCE AFTER ALL!
JUST NOT IN THE WAY I WANTED.
WE NEED TO COVER THOSE EGGS!
RAAAK

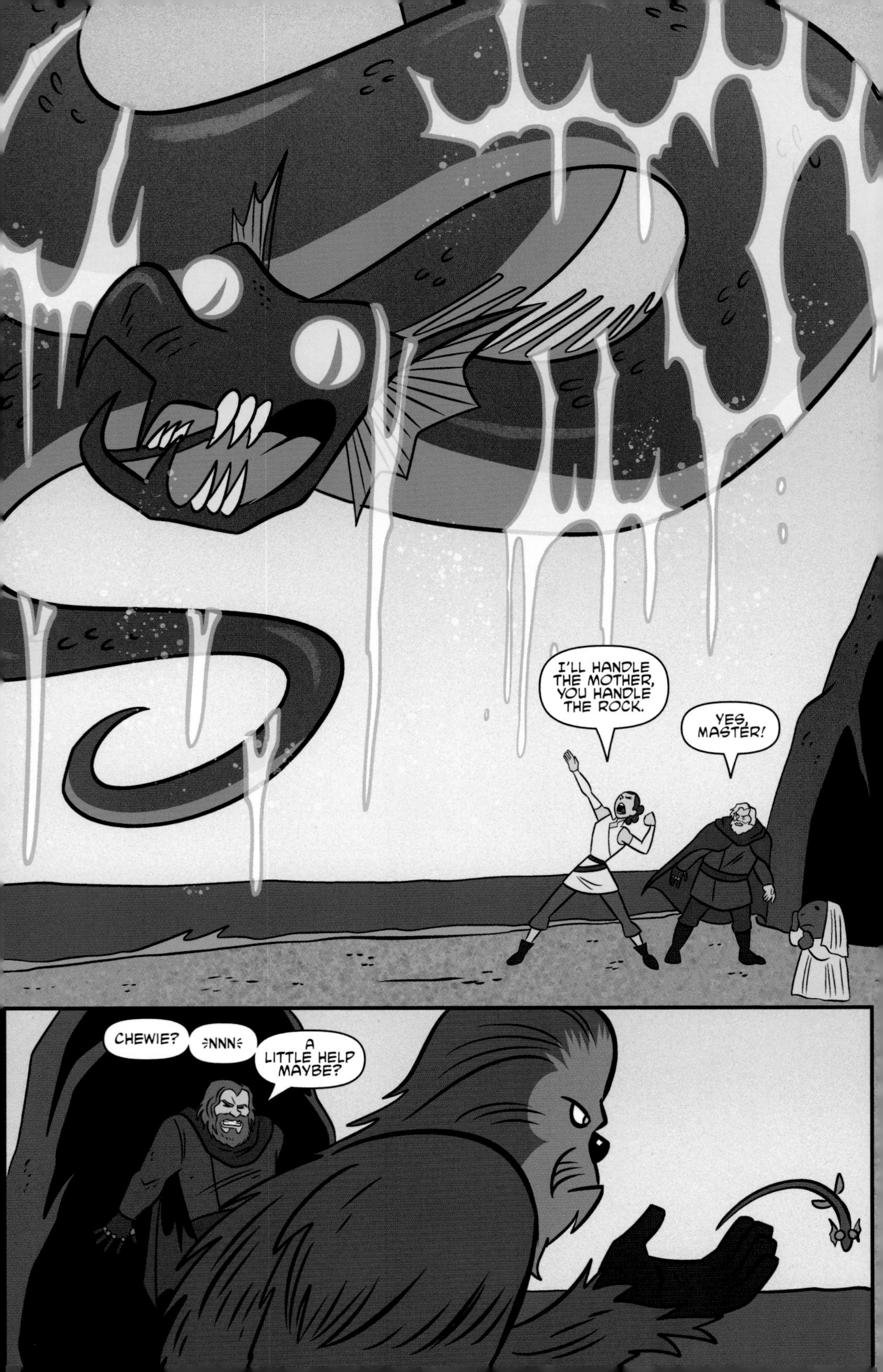
I'LL HANDLE THE MOTHER, YOU HANDLE THE ROCK.
YES, MASTER!
CHEWIE?
NNN
A LITTLE HELP MAYBE?

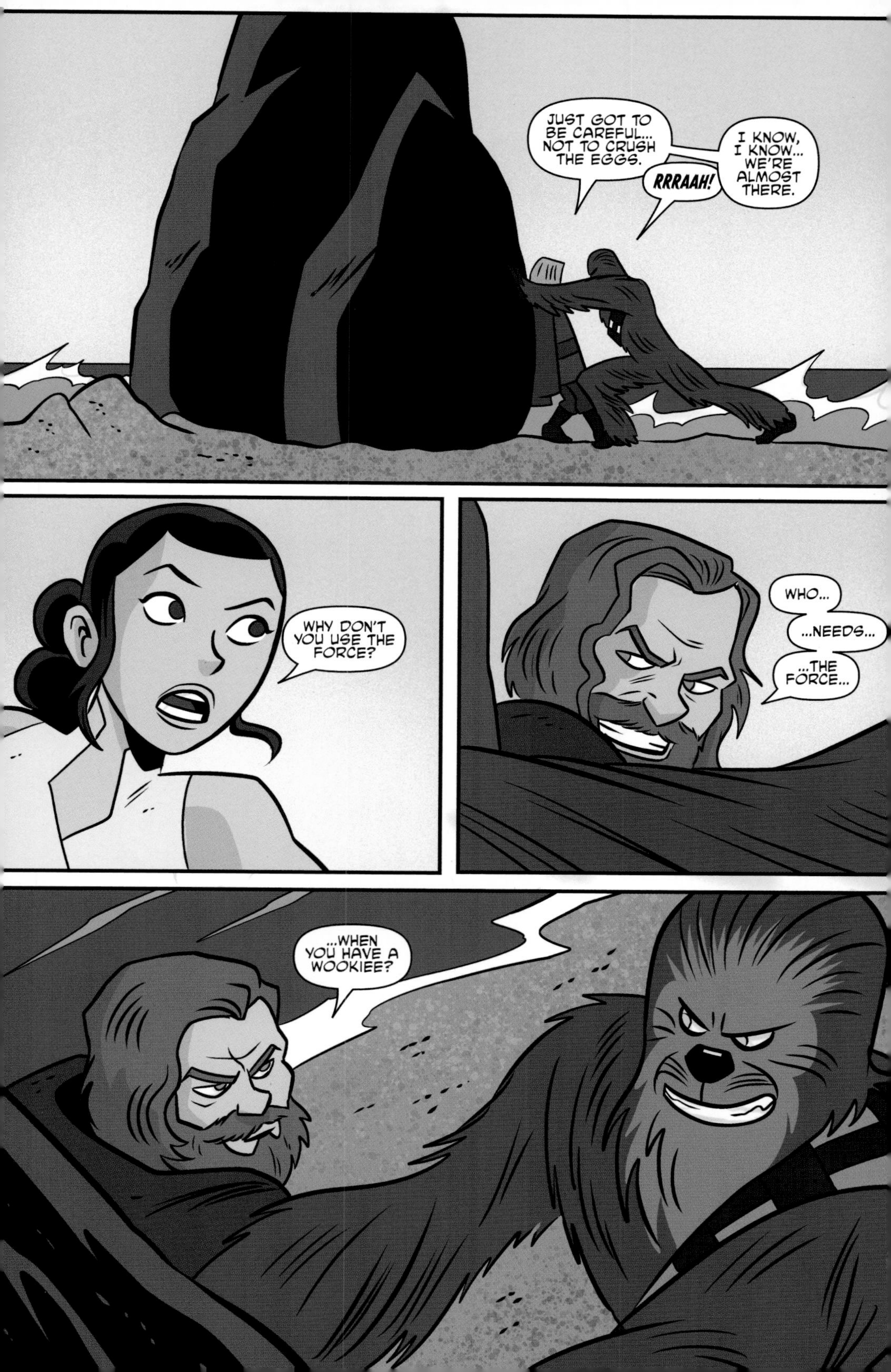
JUST GOT TO BE CAREFUL... NOT TO CRUSH THE EGGS.
RRRAAH!
I KNOW, I KNOW... WE'RE ALMOST THERE.
WHY DON'T YOU USE THE FORCE?
WHO...
...NEEDS...
...THE FORCE...
...WHEN YOU HAVE A WOOKIEE?

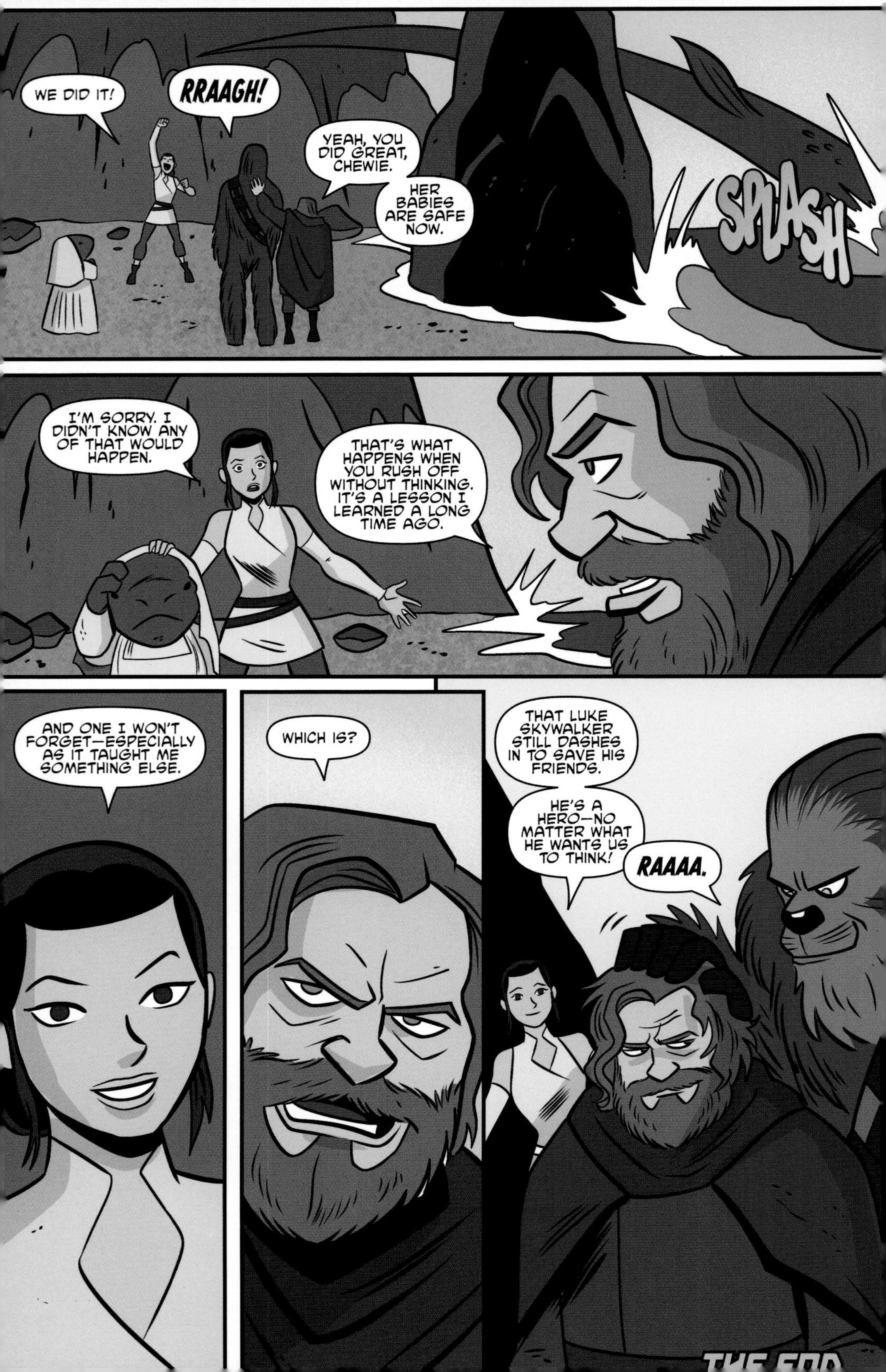
WE DID IT!
RRAAGH!
YEAH, YOU DID GREAT, CHEWIE.
HER BABIES ARE SAFE NOW.
SPLASH
I'M SORRY. I DIDN'T KNOW ANY OF THAT WOULD HAPPEN.
THAT'S WHAT HAPPENS WHEN YOU RUSH OFF WITHOUT THINKING. IT'S A LESSON I LEARNED A LONG TIME AGO.
AND ONE I WON'T FORGET—ESPECIALLY AS IT TAUGHT ME SOMETHING ELSE.
WHICH IS?
THAT LUKE SKYWALKER STILL DASHES IN TO SAVE HIS FRIENDS.
HE'S A HERO—NO MATTER WHAT HE WANTS US TO THINK!
RAAAA.

TALES FROM WILD SPACE

Win/Lose

WRITER
SHAUN HARRIS

ARTIST
MANUEL BRACCHI

COLOR FLATTER
MATT HERMS

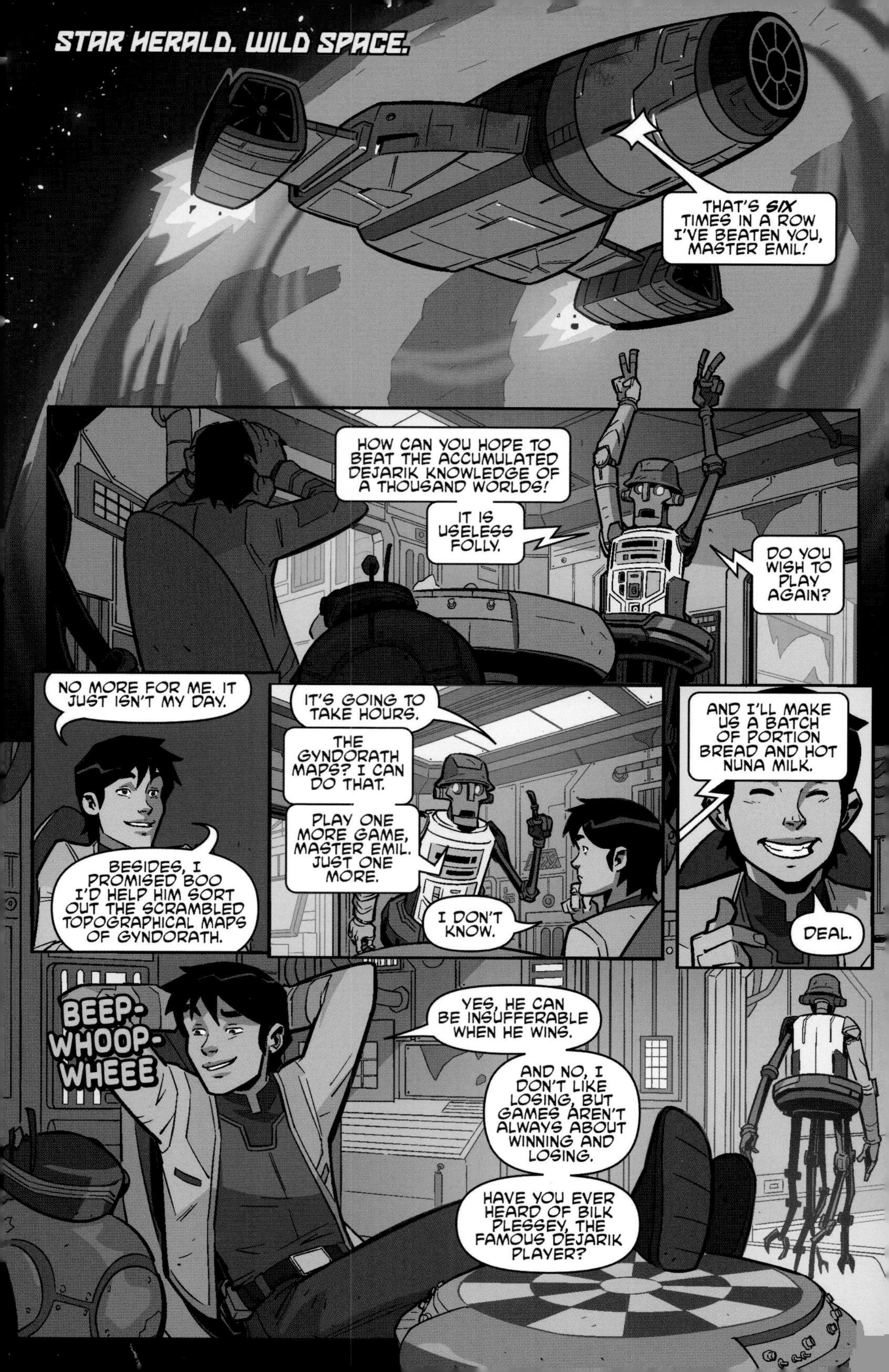
STAR HERALD. WILD SPACE.
THAT'S SIX TIMES IN A ROW I'VE BEATEN YOU, MASTER EMIL!
HOW CAN YOU HOPE TO BEAT THE ACCUMULATED DEJARIK KNOWLEDGE OF A THOUSAND WORLDS!
IT IS USELESS FOLLY.
DO YOU WISH TO PLAY AGAIN?
NO MORE FOR ME. IT JUST ISN'T MY DAY.
BESIDES, I PROMISED BOO I'D HELP HIM SORT OUT THE SCRAMBLED TOPOGRAPHICAL MAPS OF GYNDORATH.
IT'S GOING TO TAKE HOURS.
THE GYNDORATH MAPS? I CAN DO THAT.
PLAY ONE MORE GAME, MASTER EMIL. JUST ONE MORE.
I DON'T KNOW.
AND I'LL MAKE US A BATCH OF PORTION BREAD AND HOT NUNA MILK.
DEAL.
BEEP-WHOOP-WHEEE
YES, HE CAN BE INSUFFERABLE WHEN HE WINS.
AND NO, I DON'T LIKE LOSING, BUT GAMES AREN'T ALWAYS ABOUT WINNING AND LOSING.
HAVE YOU EVER HEARD OF BILK PLESSEY, THE FAMOUS DEJARIK PLAYER?

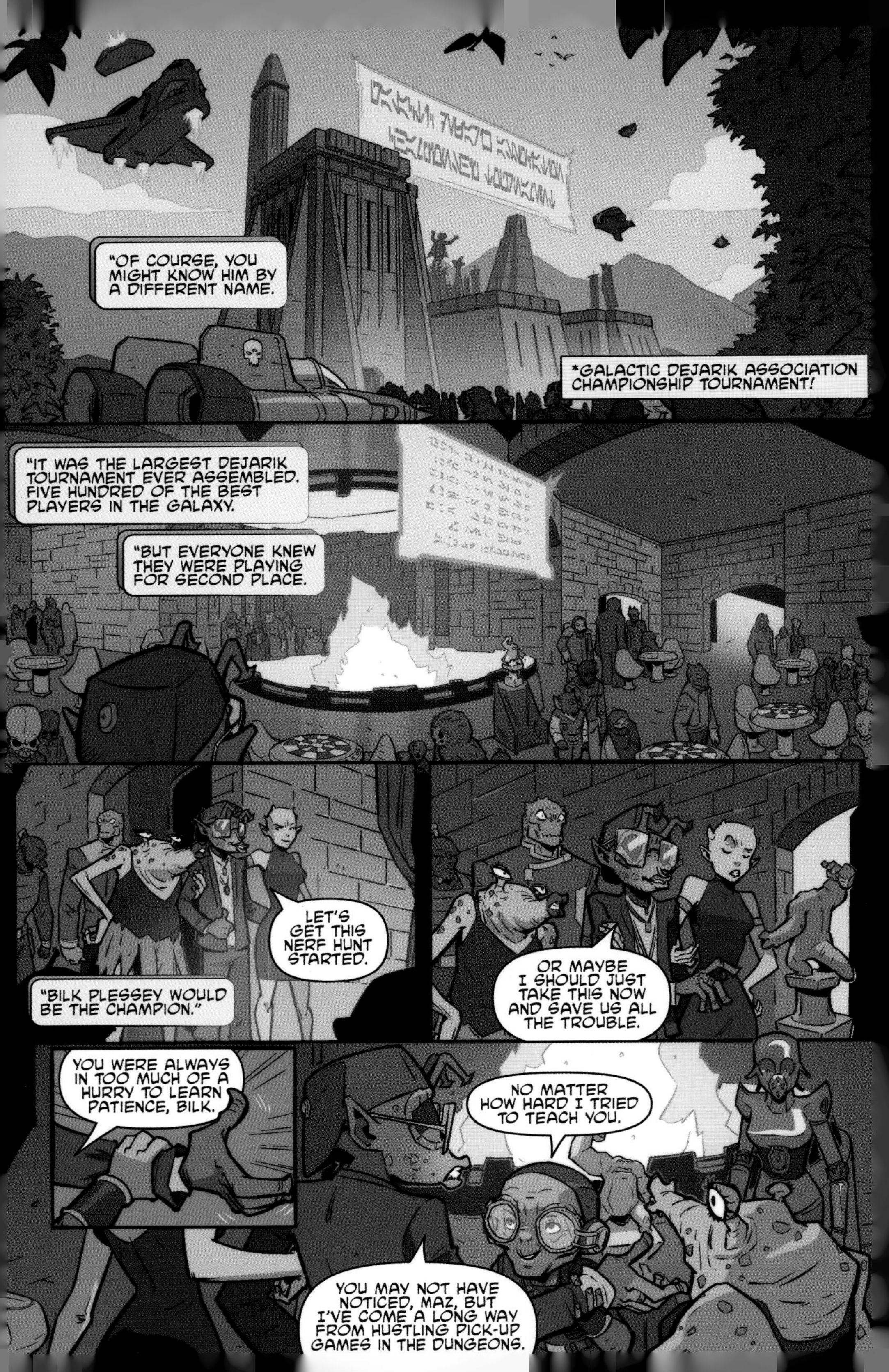
"OF COURSE, YOU MIGHT KNOW HIM BY A DIFFERENT NAME.
*GALACTIC DEJARIK ASSOCIATION CHAMPIONSHIP TOURNAMENT!
"IT WAS THE LARGEST DEJARIK TOURNAMENT EVER ASSEMBLED. FIVE HUNDRED OF THE BEST PLAYERS IN THE GALAXY.
"BUT EVERYONE KNEW THEY WERE PLAYING FOR SECOND PLACE.
LET'S GET THIS NERF HUNT STARTED.
"BILK PLESSEY WOULD BE THE CHAMPION."
OR MAYBE I SHOULD JUST TAKE THIS NOW AND SAVE US ALL THE TROUBLE.
YOU WERE ALWAYS IN TOO MUCH OF A HURRY TO LEARN PATIENCE, BILK.
NO MATTER HOW HARD I TRIED TO TEACH YOU.
YOU MAY NOT HAVE NOTICED, MAZ, BUT I'VE COME A LONG WAY FROM HUSTLING PICK-UP GAMES IN THE DUNGEONS.

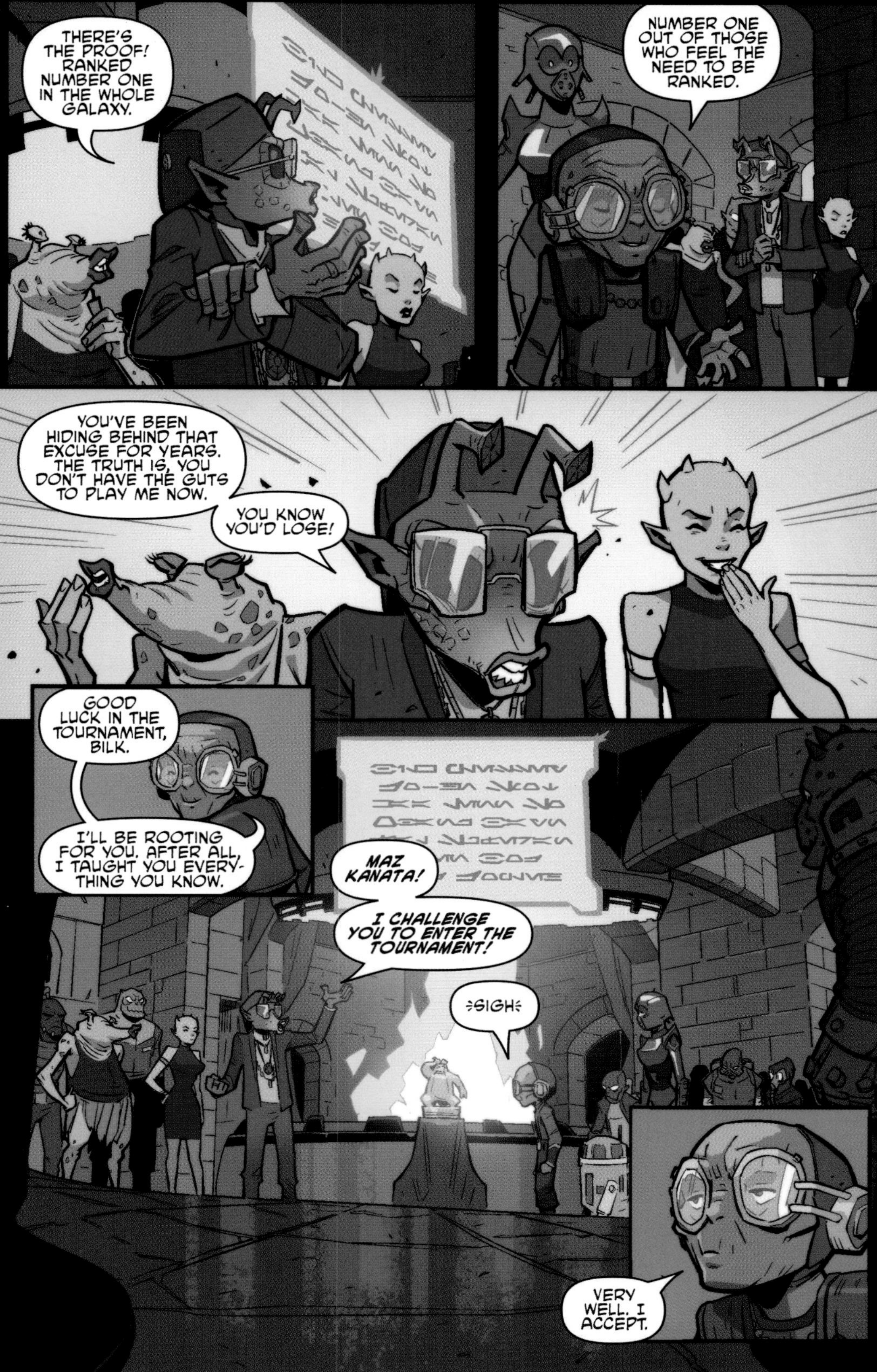
THERE'S THE PROOF! RANKED NUMBER ONE IN THE WHOLE GALAXY.
NUMBER ONE OUT OF THOSE WHO FEEL THE NEED TO BE RANKED.
YOU'VE BEEN HIDING BEHIND THAT EXCUSE FOR YEARS. THE TRUTH IS, YOU DON'T HAVE THE GUTS TO PLAY ME NOW.
YOU KNOW YOU'D LOSE!
GOOD LUCK IN THE TOURNAMENT, BILK.
I'LL BE ROOTING FOR YOU. AFTER ALL, I TAUGHT YOU EVERY-THING YOU KNOW.
MAZ KANATA!
I CHALLENGE YOU TO ENTER THE TOURNAMENT!
SIGH
VERY WELL. I ACCEPT.

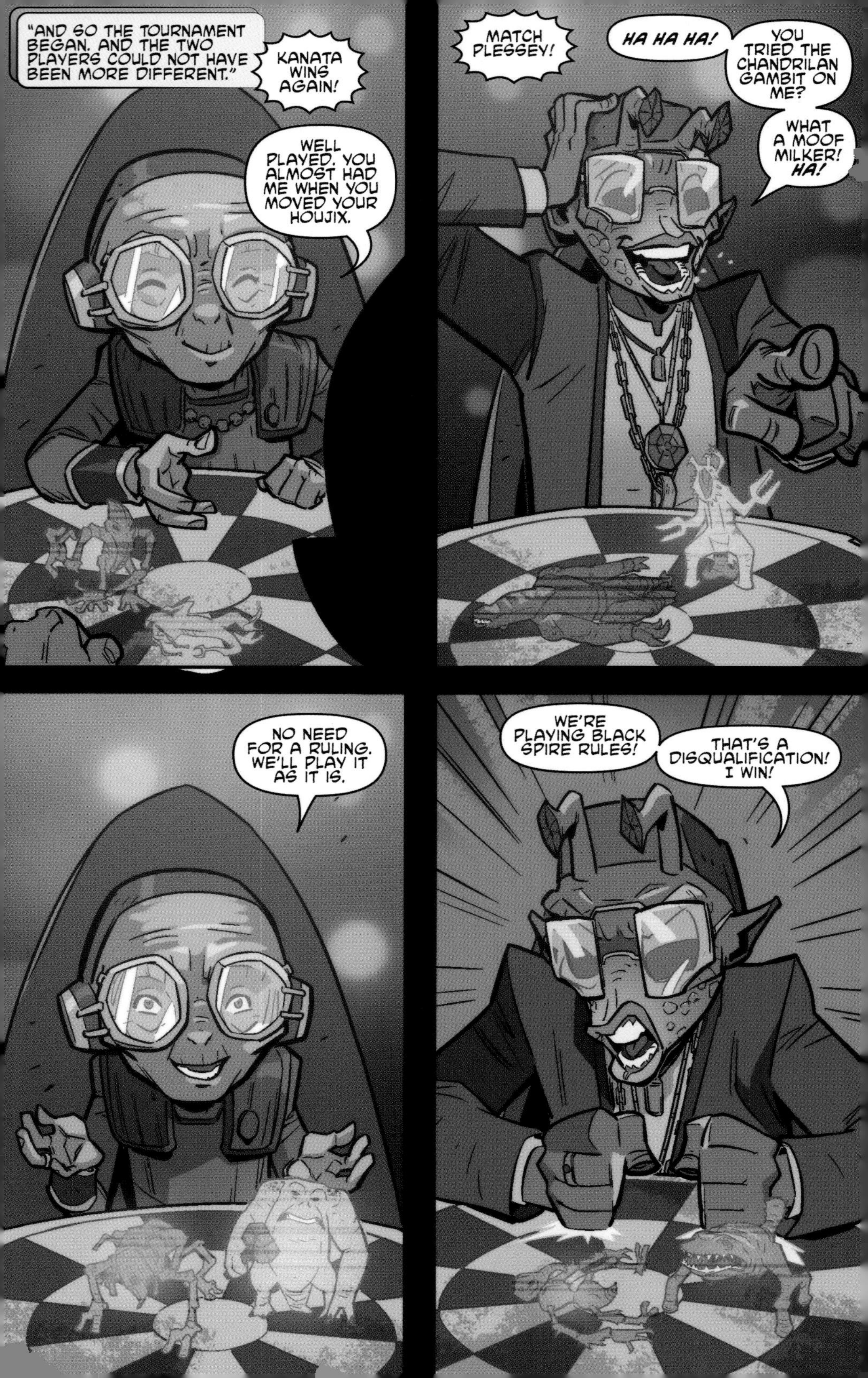
"AND SO THE TOURNAMENT BEGAN. AND THE TWO PLAYERS COULD NOT HAVE BEEN MORE DIFFERENT."
KANATA WINS AGAIN!
WELL PLAYED. YOU ALMOST HAD ME WHEN YOU MOVED YOUR HOUJIX.
MATCH PLESSEY!
HA HA HA!
YOU TRIED THE CHANDRILAN GAMBIT ON ME?
WHAT A MOOF MILKER! HA!
NO NEED FOR A RULING. WE'LL PLAY IT AS IT IS.
WE'RE PLAYING BLACK SPIRE RULES!
THAT'S A DISQUALIFICATION! I WIN!

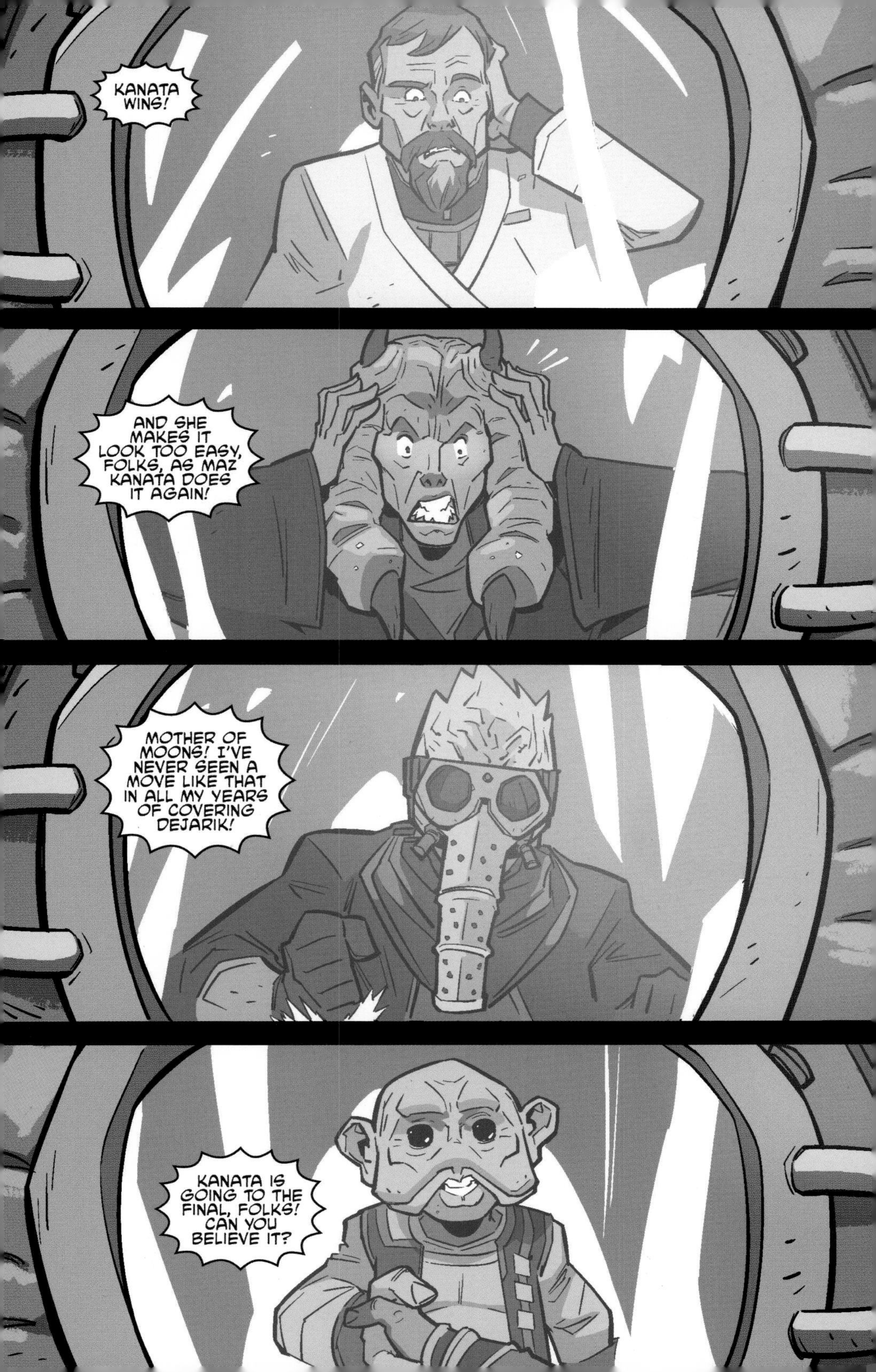
KANATA WINS!
AND SHE MAKES IT LOOK TOO EASY, FOLKS, AS MAZ KANATA DOES IT AGAIN!
MOTHER OF MOONS! I'VE NEVER SEEN A MOVE LIKE THAT IN ALL MY YEARS OF COVERING DEJARIK!
KANATA IS GOING TO THE FINAL, FOLKS! CAN YOU BELIEVE IT?

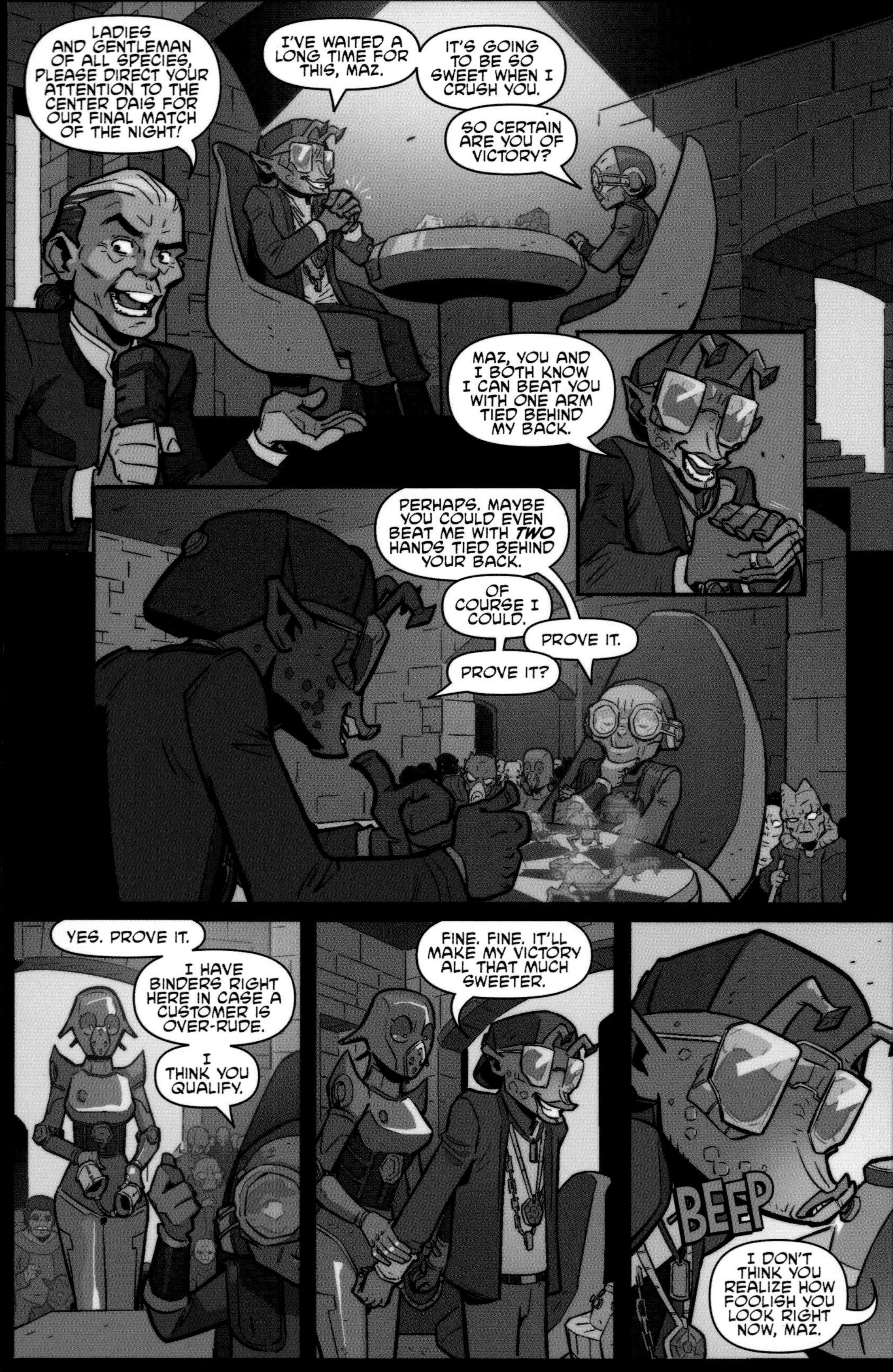
LADIES AND GENTLEMAN OF ALL SPECIES, PLEASE DIRECT YOUR ATTENTION TO THE CENTER DAIS FOR OUR FINAL MATCH OF THE NIGHT!
I'VE WAITED A LONG TIME FOR THIS, MAZ.
IT'S GOING TO BE SO SWEET WHEN I CRUSH YOU.
SO CERTAIN ARE YOU OF VICTORY?
MAZ, YOU AND I BOTH KNOW I CAN BEAT YOU WITH ONE ARM TIED BEHIND MY BACK.
PERHAPS. MAYBE YOU COULD EVEN BEAT ME WITH *TWO* HANDS TIED BEHIND YOUR BACK.
OF COURSE I COULD.
PROVE IT.
PROVE IT?
YES. PROVE IT.
I HAVE BINDERS RIGHT HERE IN CASE A CUSTOMER IS OVER-RUDE.
I THINK YOU QUALIFY.
FINE. FINE. IT'LL MAKE MY VICTORY ALL THAT MUCH SWEETER.
BEEP
I DON'T THINK YOU REALIZE HOW FOOLISH YOU LOOK RIGHT NOW, MAZ.

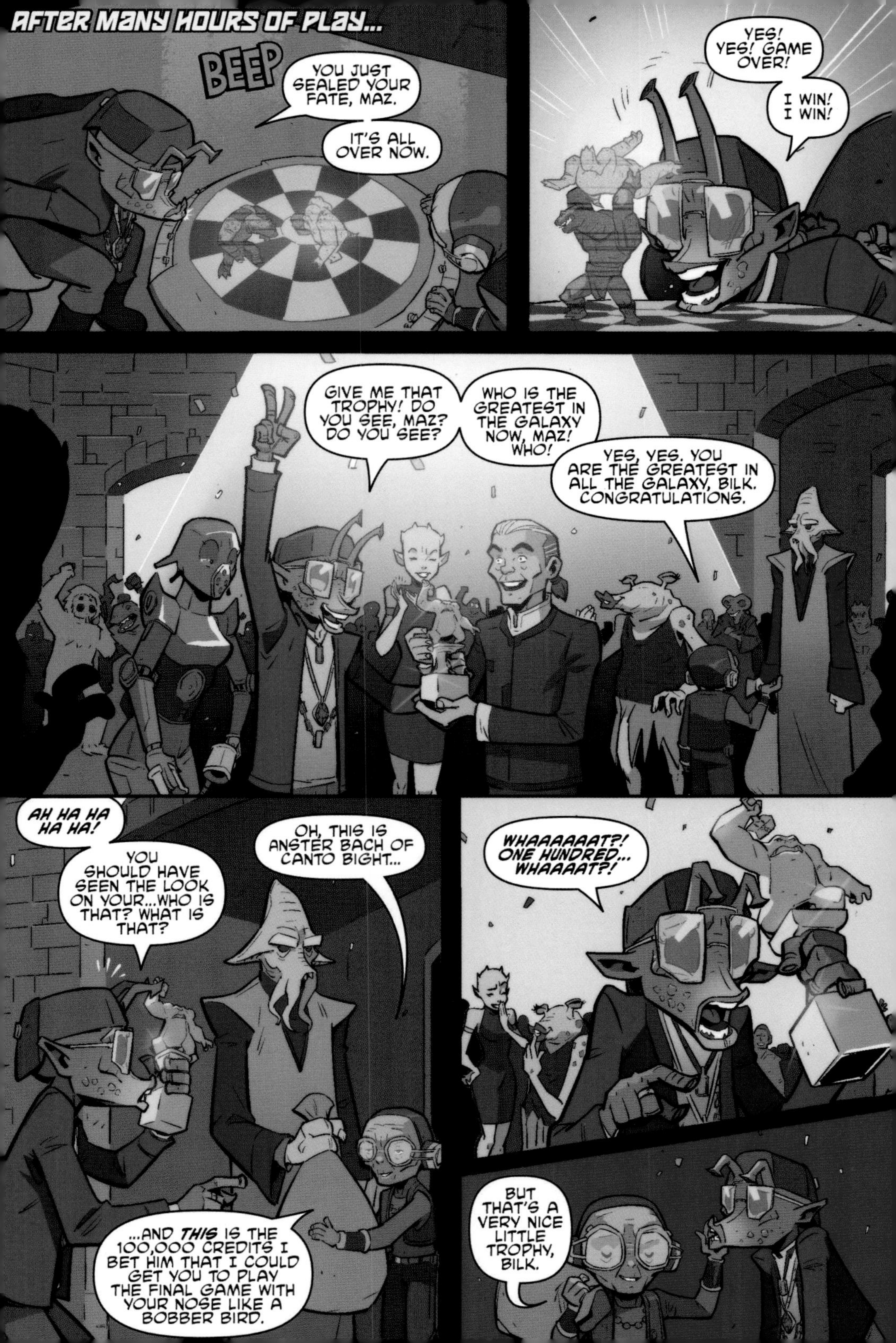
AFTER MANY HOURS OF PLAY...
BEEP
YOU JUST SEALED YOUR FATE, MAZ.
IT'S ALL OVER NOW.
YES! YES! GAME OVER!
I WIN! I WIN!
GIVE ME THAT TROPHY! DO YOU SEE, MAZ? DO YOU SEE?
WHO IS THE GREATEST IN THE GALAXY NOW, MAZ! WHO!
YES, YES. YOU ARE THE GREATEST IN ALL THE GALAXY, BILK. CONGRATULATIONS.
AH HA HA HA HA!
YOU SHOULD HAVE SEEN THE LOOK ON YOUR...WHO IS THAT? WHAT IS THAT?
OH, THIS IS ANSTER BACH OF CANTO BIGHT...
...AND THIS IS THE 100,000 CREDITS I BET HIM THAT I COULD GET YOU TO PLAY THE FINAL GAME WITH YOUR NOSE LIKE A BOBBER BIRD.
WHAAAAAAT?! ONE HUNDRED... WHAAAAT?!
BUT THAT'S A VERY NICE LITTLE TROPHY, BILK.

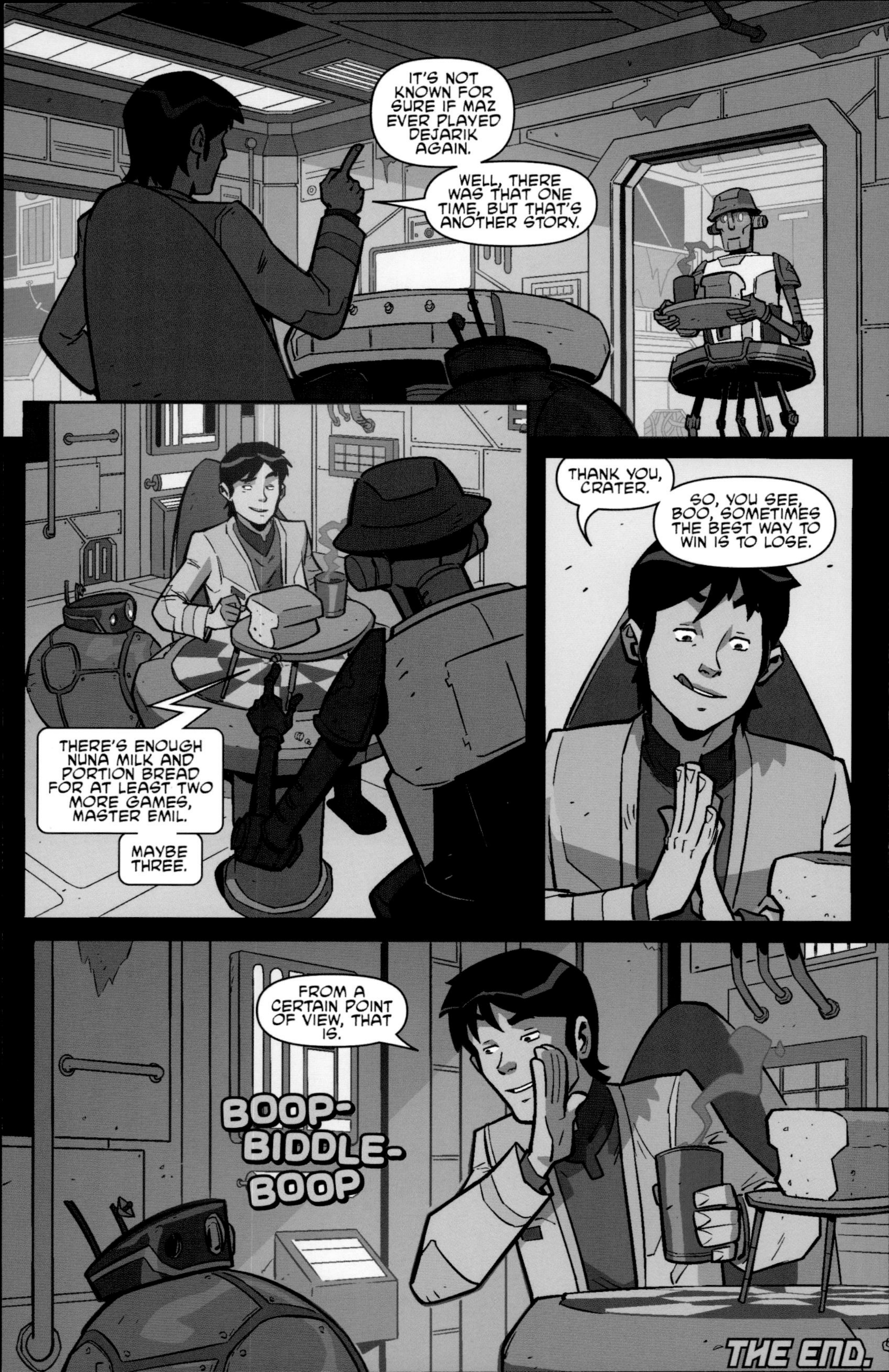
IT'S NOT KNOWN FOR SURE IF MAZ EVER PLAYED DEJARIK AGAIN.
WELL, THERE WAS THAT ONE TIME, BUT THAT'S ANOTHER STORY.
THERE'S ENOUGH NUNA MILK AND PORTION BREAD FOR AT LEAST TWO MORE GAMES, MASTER EMIL.
MAYBE THREE.
THANK YOU, CRATER.
SO, YOU SEE, BOO, SOMETIMES THE BEST WAY TO WIN IS TO LOSE.
FROM A CERTAIN POINT OF VIEW, THAT IS.
BOOP-BIDDLE-BOOP
THE END.

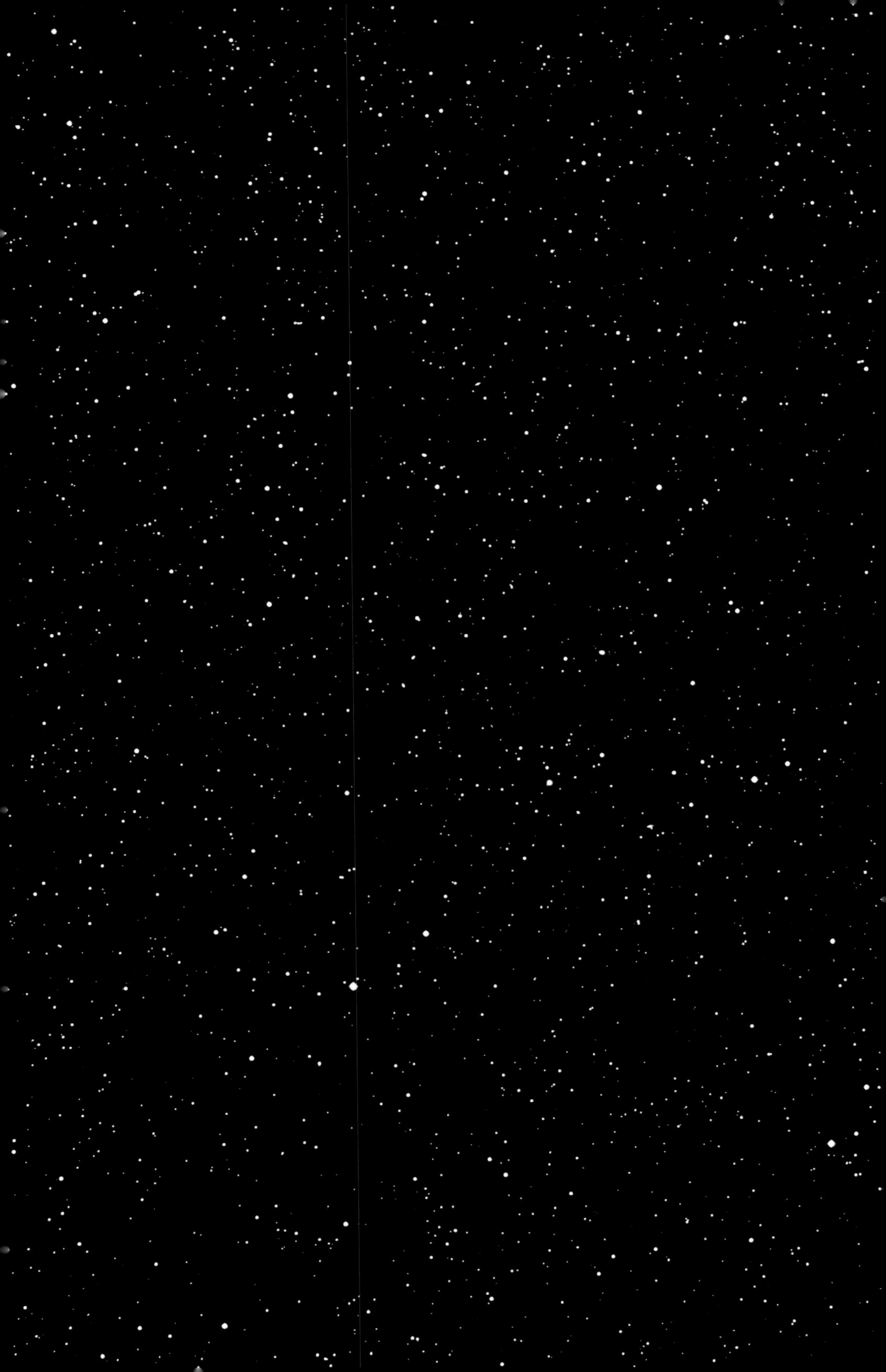

TALES FROM WILD SPACE

Alone in the Dark

WRITER
ADAM CHRISTOPHER

ARTIST
MEGAN LEVENS

COLORIST
CHARLIE KIRCHOFF

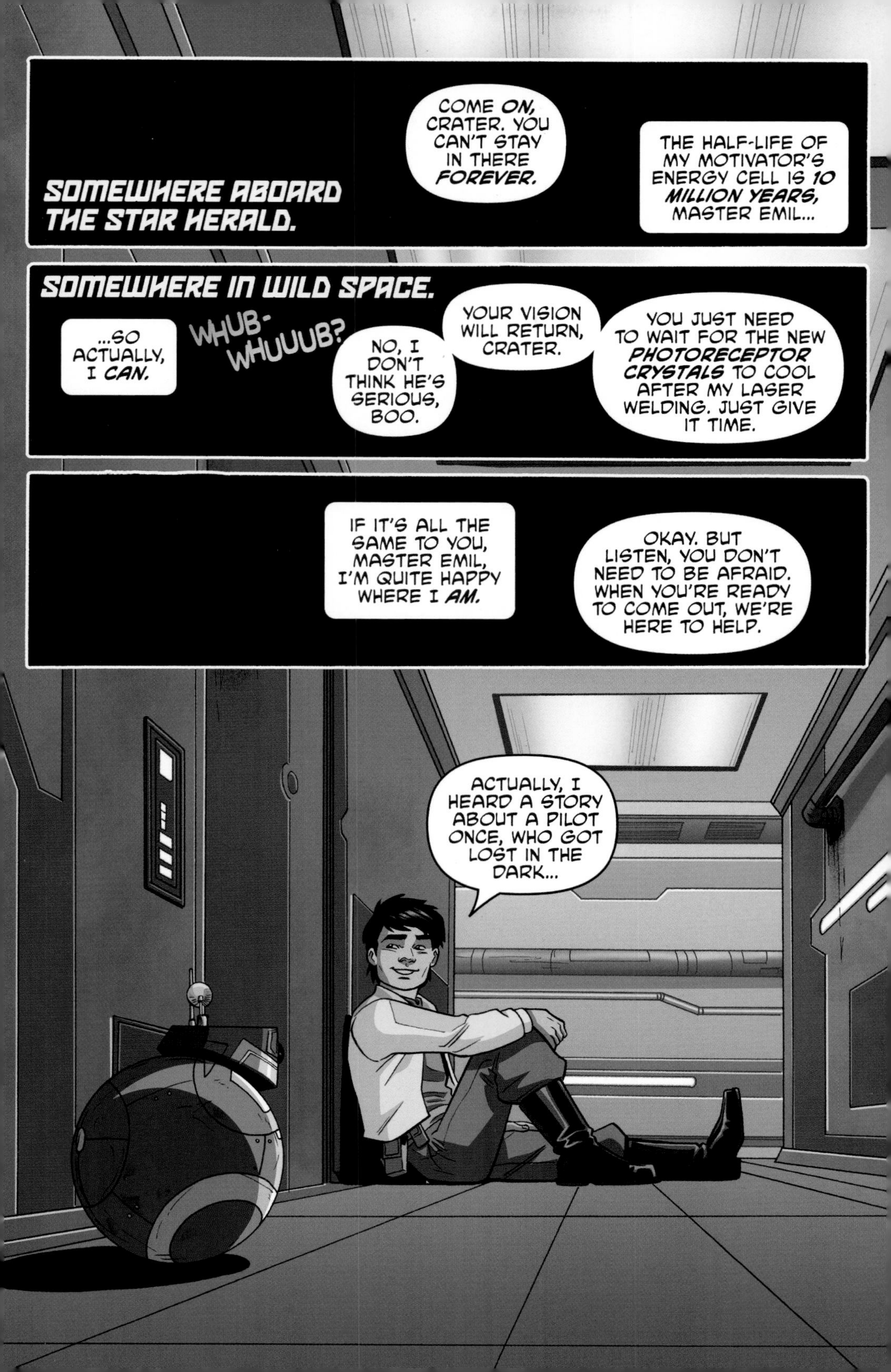

SOMEWHERE ABOARD THE STAR HERALD.
COME ON, CRATER. YOU CAN'T STAY IN THERE FOREVER.
THE HALF-LIFE OF MY MOTIVATOR'S ENERGY CELL IS 10 MILLION YEARS, MASTER EMIL...
SOMEWHERE IN WILD SPACE.
...SO ACTUALLY, I CAN.
WHUB-WHUUUB?
NO, I DON'T THINK HE'S SERIOUS, BOO.
YOUR VISION WILL RETURN, CRATER.
YOU JUST NEED TO WAIT FOR THE NEW PHOTORECEPTOR CRYSTALS TO COOL AFTER MY LASER WELDING. JUST GIVE IT TIME.
IF IT'S ALL THE SAME TO YOU, MASTER EMIL, I'M QUITE HAPPY WHERE I AM.
OKAY. BUT LISTEN, YOU DON'T NEED TO BE AFRAID. WHEN YOU'RE READY TO COME OUT, WE'RE HERE TO HELP.
ACTUALLY, I HEARD A STORY ABOUT A PILOT ONCE, WHO GOT LOST IN THE DARK...

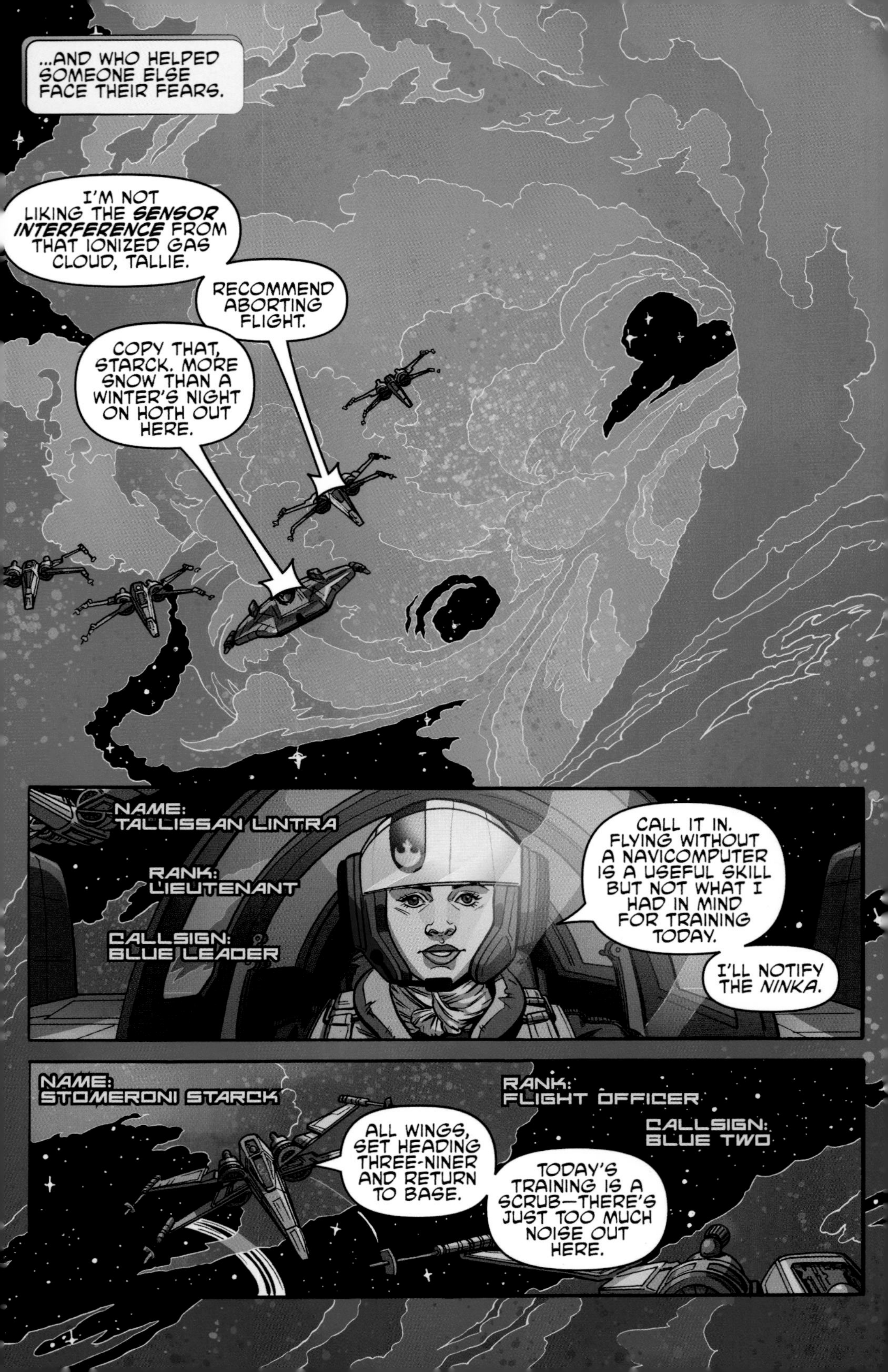
...AND WHO HELPED SOMEONE ELSE FACE THEIR FEARS.
I'M NOT LIKING THE SENSOR INTERFERENCE FROM THAT IONIZED GAS CLOUD, TALLIE.
RECOMMEND ABORTING FLIGHT.
COPY THAT, STARCK. MORE SNOW THAN A WINTER'S NIGHT ON HOTH OUT HERE.
NAME: TALLISSAN LINTRA
RANK: LIEUTENANT
CALLSIGN: BLUE LEADER
CALL IT IN. FLYING WITHOUT A NAVICOMPUTER IS A USEFUL SKILL BUT NOT WHAT I HAD IN MIND FOR TRAINING TODAY.
I'LL NOTIFY THE NINKA.
NAME: STOMERONI STARCK
RANK: FLIGHT OFFICER
CALLSIGN: BLUE TWO
ALL WINGS, SET HEADING THREE-NINER AND RETURN TO BASE.
TODAY'S TRAINING IS A SCRUB—THERE'S JUST TOO MUCH NOISE OUT HERE.

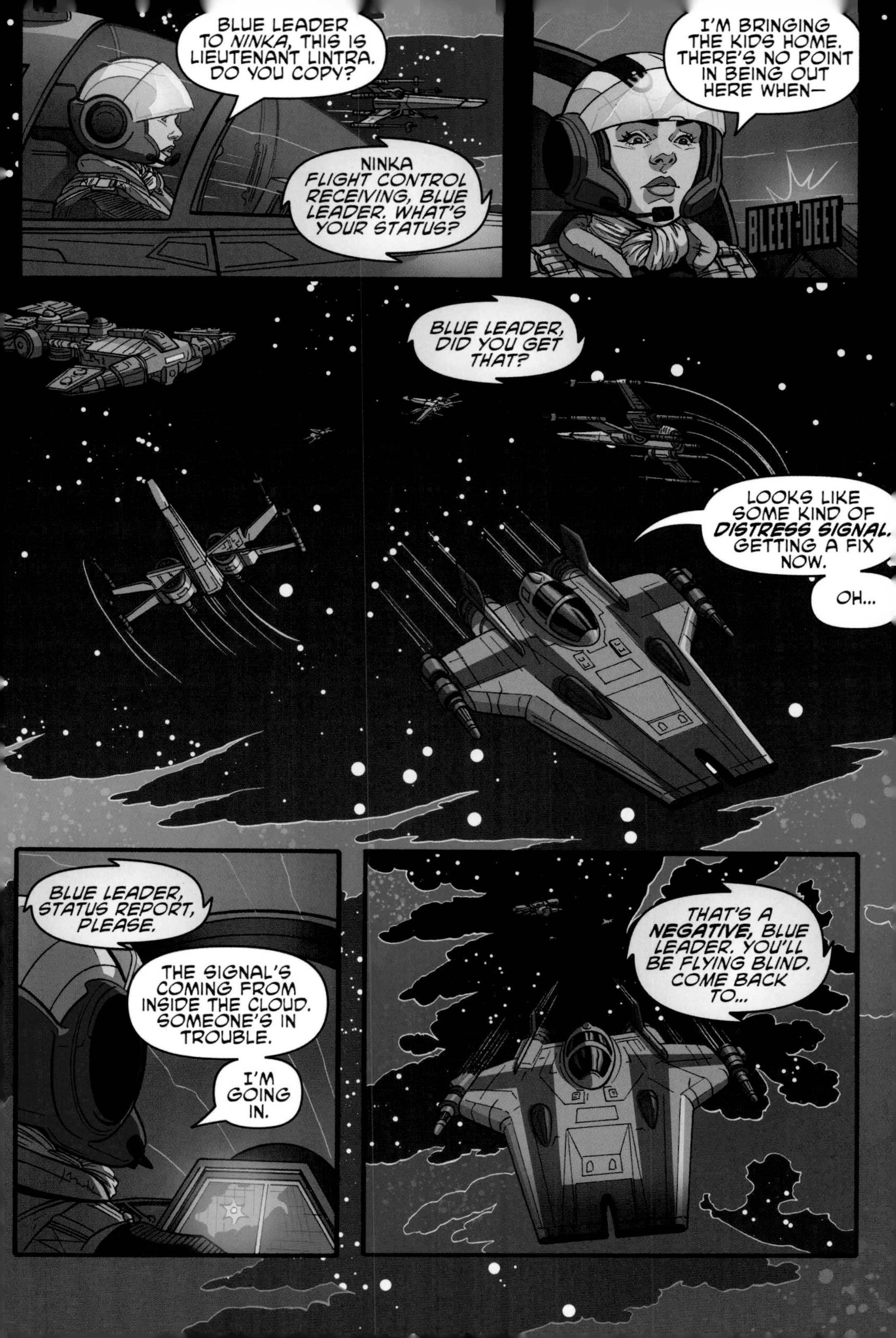
BLUE LEADER TO *NINKA*, THIS IS LIEUTENANT LINTRA. DO YOU COPY?
NINKA FLIGHT CONTROL RECEIVING, BLUE LEADER. WHAT'S YOUR STATUS?
I'M BRINGING THE KIDS HOME. THERE'S NO POINT IN BEING OUT HERE WHEN—
BLEET-DEET
BLUE LEADER, DID YOU GET THAT?
LOOKS LIKE SOME KIND OF ***DISTRESS SIGNAL.*** GETTING A FIX NOW.
OH...
BLUE LEADER, STATUS REPORT, PLEASE.
THE SIGNAL'S COMING FROM INSIDE THE CLOUD. SOMEONE'S IN TROUBLE.
I'M GOING IN.
THAT'S A ***NEGATIVE,*** BLUE LEADER. YOU'LL BE FLYING BLIND. COME BACK TO...

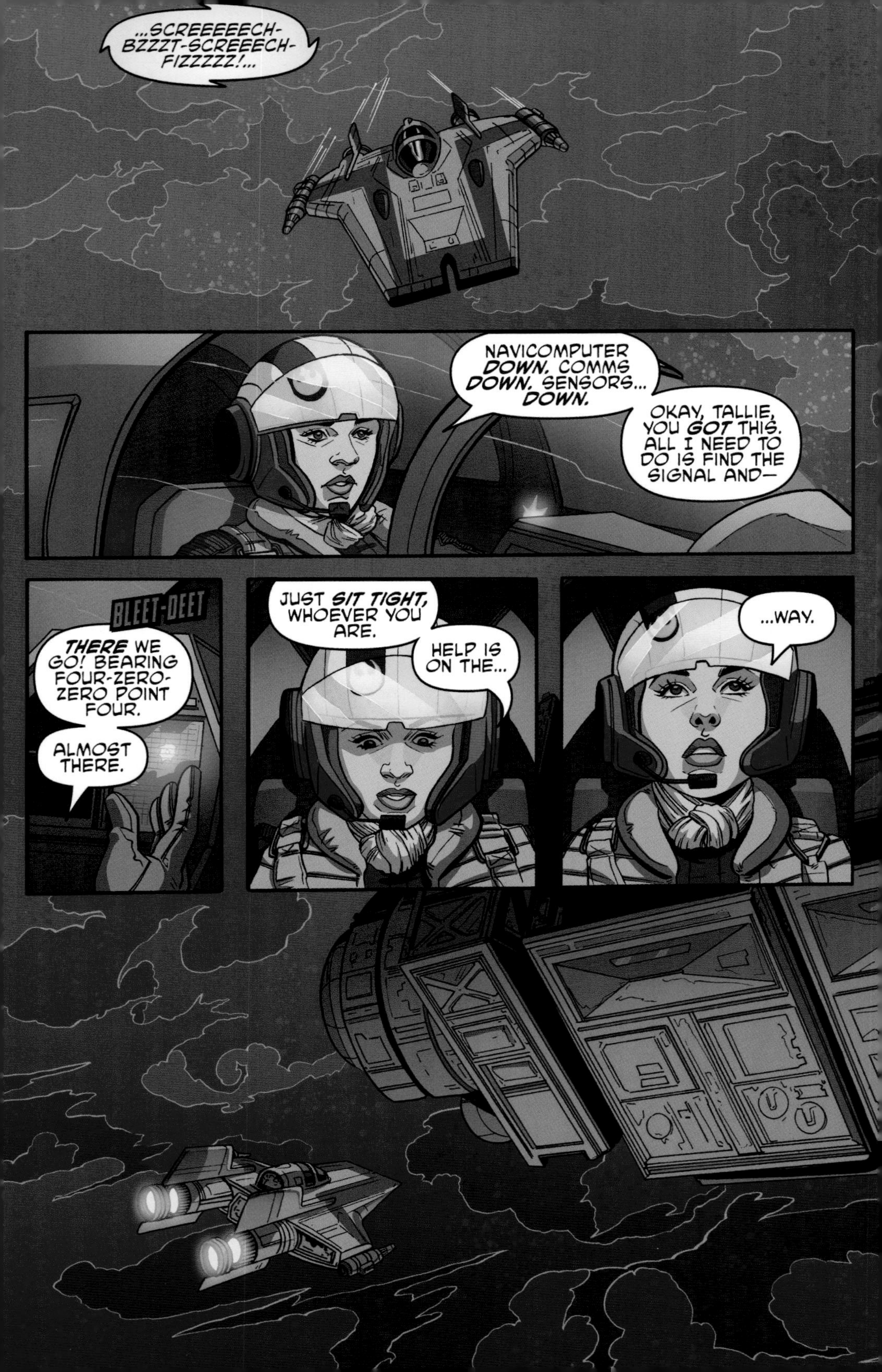

...SCREEEEECH-BZZZT-SCREEECH-FIZZZZZ!...
NAVICOMPUTER DOWN. COMMS DOWN. SENSORS... DOWN.
OKAY, TALLIE, YOU GOT THIS. ALL I NEED TO DO IS FIND THE SIGNAL AND—
BLEET-DEET
THERE WE GO! BEARING FOUR-ZERO-ZERO POINT FOUR.
ALMOST THERE.
JUST SIT TIGHT, WHOEVER YOU ARE.
HELP IS ON THE...
...WAY.

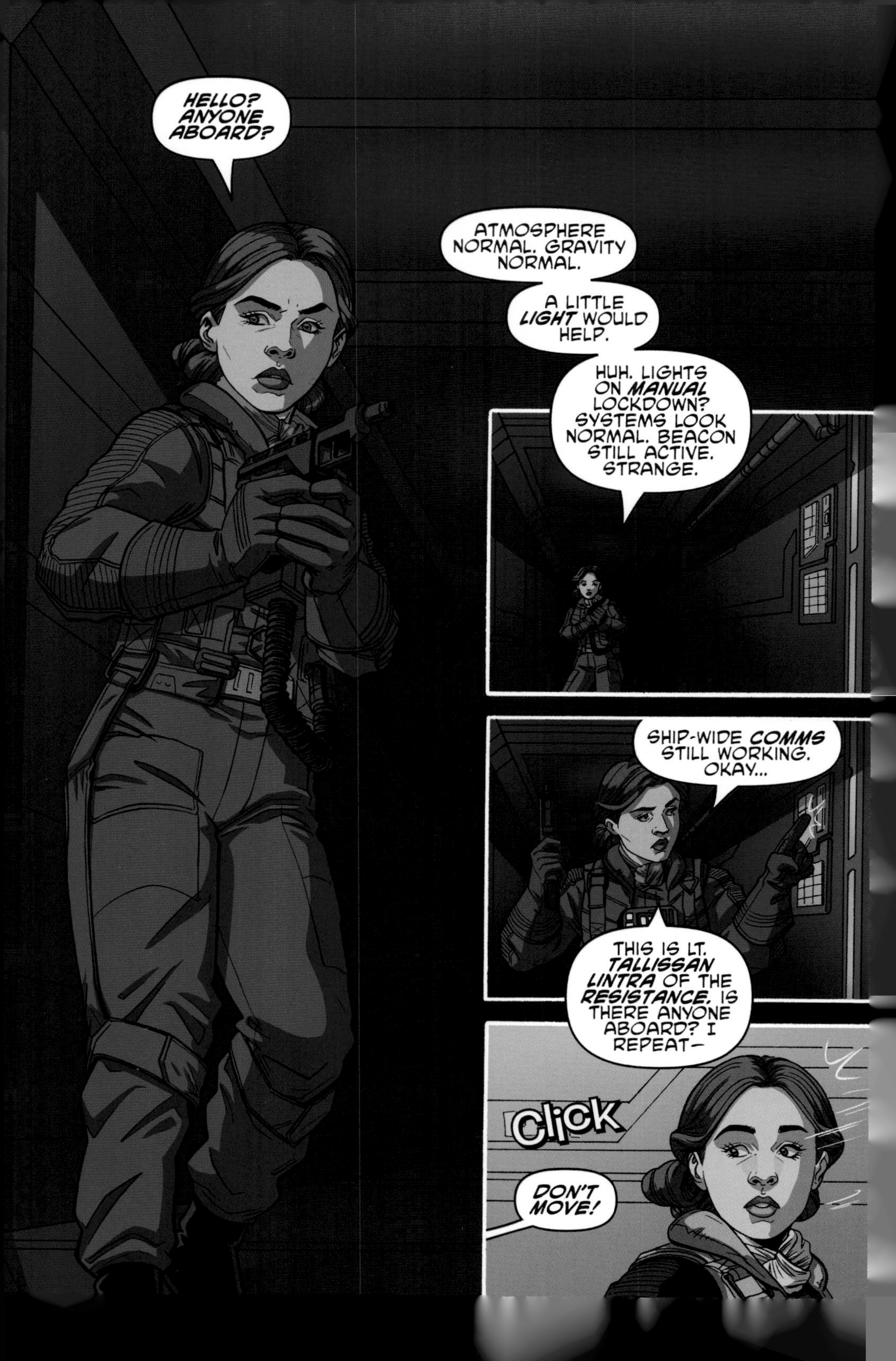
HELLO? ANYONE ABOARD?
ATMOSPHERE NORMAL. GRAVITY NORMAL.
A LITTLE LIGHT WOULD HELP.
HUH. LIGHTS ON MANUAL LOCKDOWN? SYSTEMS LOOK NORMAL. BEACON STILL ACTIVE. STRANGE.
SHIP-WIDE COMMS STILL WORKING. OKAY...
THIS IS LT. TALLISSAN LINTRA OF THE RESISTANCE. IS THERE ANYONE ABOARD? I REPEAT—
CLICK
DON'T MOVE!

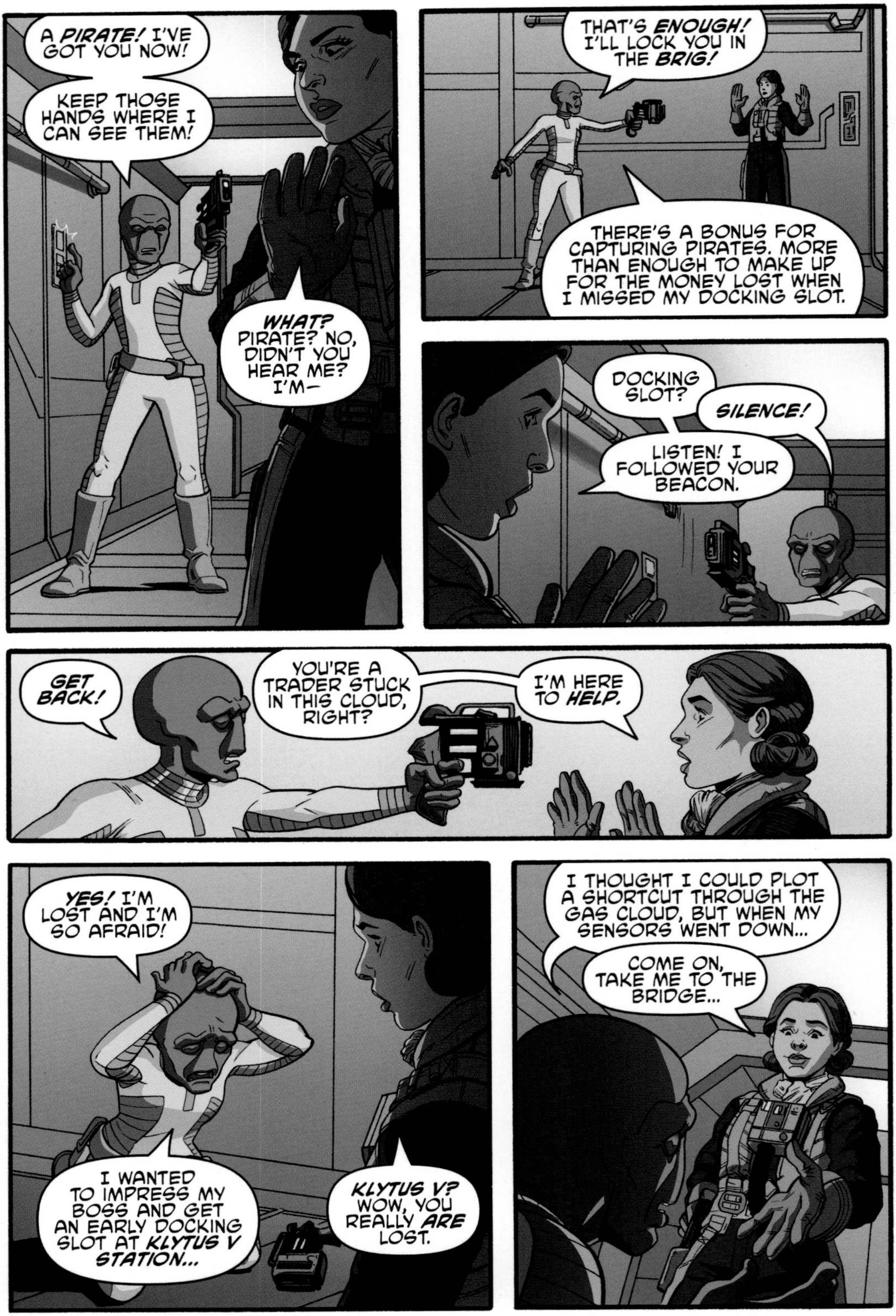
A PIRATE! I'VE GOT YOU NOW!
KEEP THOSE HANDS WHERE I CAN SEE THEM!
WHAT? PIRATE? NO, DIDN'T YOU HEAR ME? I'M—
THAT'S ENOUGH! I'LL LOCK YOU IN THE BRIG!
THERE'S A BONUS FOR CAPTURING PIRATES. MORE THAN ENOUGH TO MAKE UP FOR THE MONEY LOST WHEN I MISSED MY DOCKING SLOT.
DOCKING SLOT?
SILENCE!
LISTEN! I FOLLOWED YOUR BEACON.
GET BACK!
YOU'RE A TRADER STUCK IN THIS CLOUD, RIGHT?
I'M HERE TO HELP.
YES! I'M LOST AND I'M SO AFRAID!
I WANTED TO IMPRESS MY BOSS AND GET AN EARLY DOCKING SLOT AT KLYTUS V STATION...
KLYTUS V? WOW, YOU REALLY ARE LOST.
I THOUGHT I COULD PLOT A SHORTCUT THROUGH THE GAS CLOUD, BUT WHEN MY SENSORS WENT DOWN...
COME ON, TAKE ME TO THE BRIDGE...

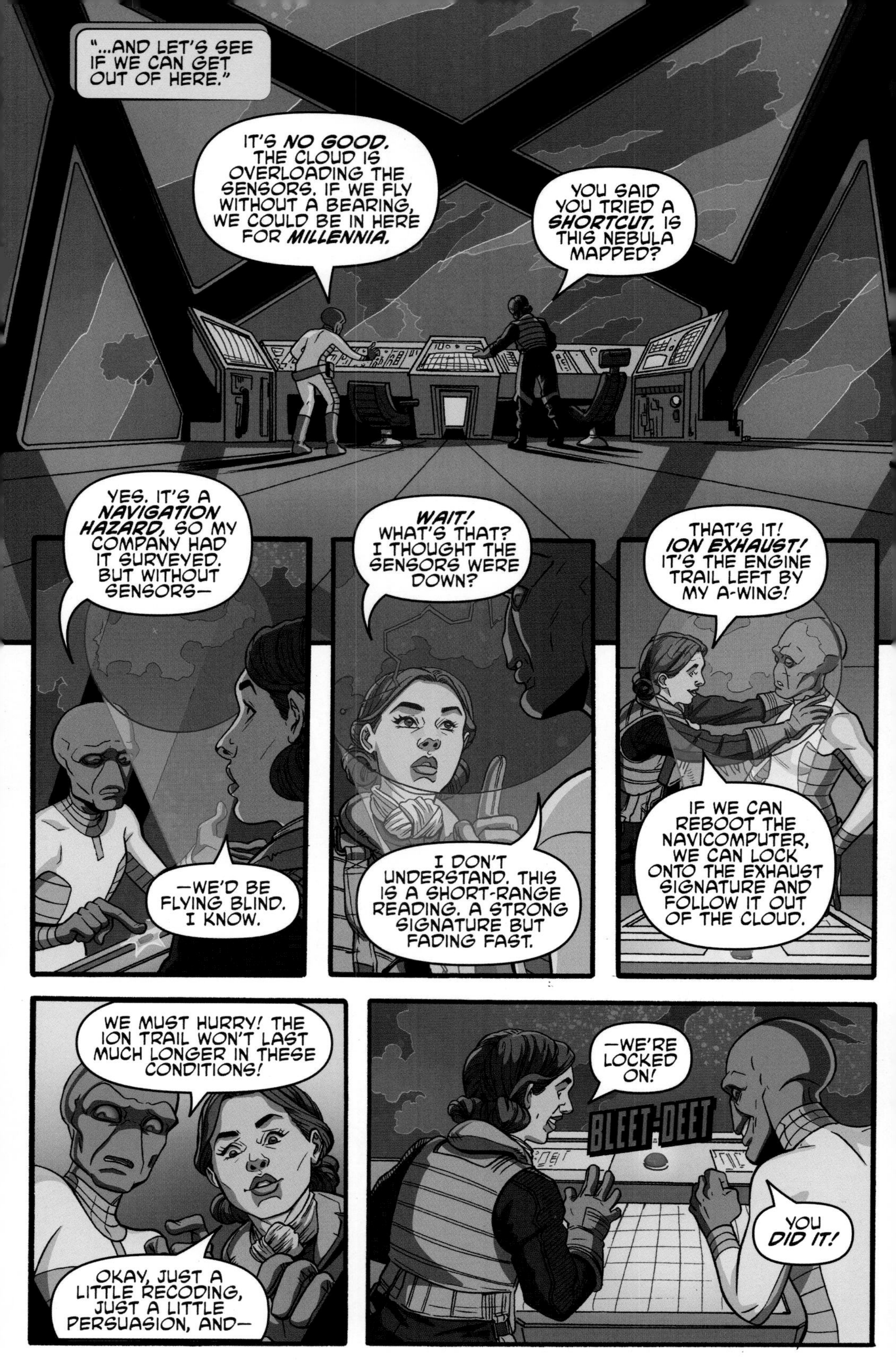
"...AND LET'S SEE IF WE CAN GET OUT OF HERE."
IT'S NO GOOD. THE CLOUD IS OVERLOADING THE SENSORS. IF WE FLY WITHOUT A BEARING, WE COULD BE IN HERE FOR MILLENNIA.
YOU SAID YOU TRIED A SHORTCUT. IS THIS NEBULA MAPPED?
YES. IT'S A NAVIGATION HAZARD, SO MY COMPANY HAD IT SURVEYED. BUT WITHOUT SENSORS—
—WE'D BE FLYING BLIND. I KNOW.
WAIT! WHAT'S THAT? I THOUGHT THE SENSORS WERE DOWN?
I DON'T UNDERSTAND. THIS IS A SHORT-RANGE READING. A STRONG SIGNATURE BUT FADING FAST.
THAT'S IT! ION EXHAUST! IT'S THE ENGINE TRAIL LEFT BY MY A-WING!
IF WE CAN REBOOT THE NAVICOMPUTER, WE CAN LOCK ONTO THE EXHAUST SIGNATURE AND FOLLOW IT OUT OF THE CLOUD.
WE MUST HURRY! THE ION TRAIL WON'T LAST MUCH LONGER IN THESE CONDITIONS!
OKAY, JUST A LITTLE RECODING, JUST A LITTLE PERSUASION, AND—
—WE'RE LOCKED ON!
BLEET-DEET
YOU DID IT!

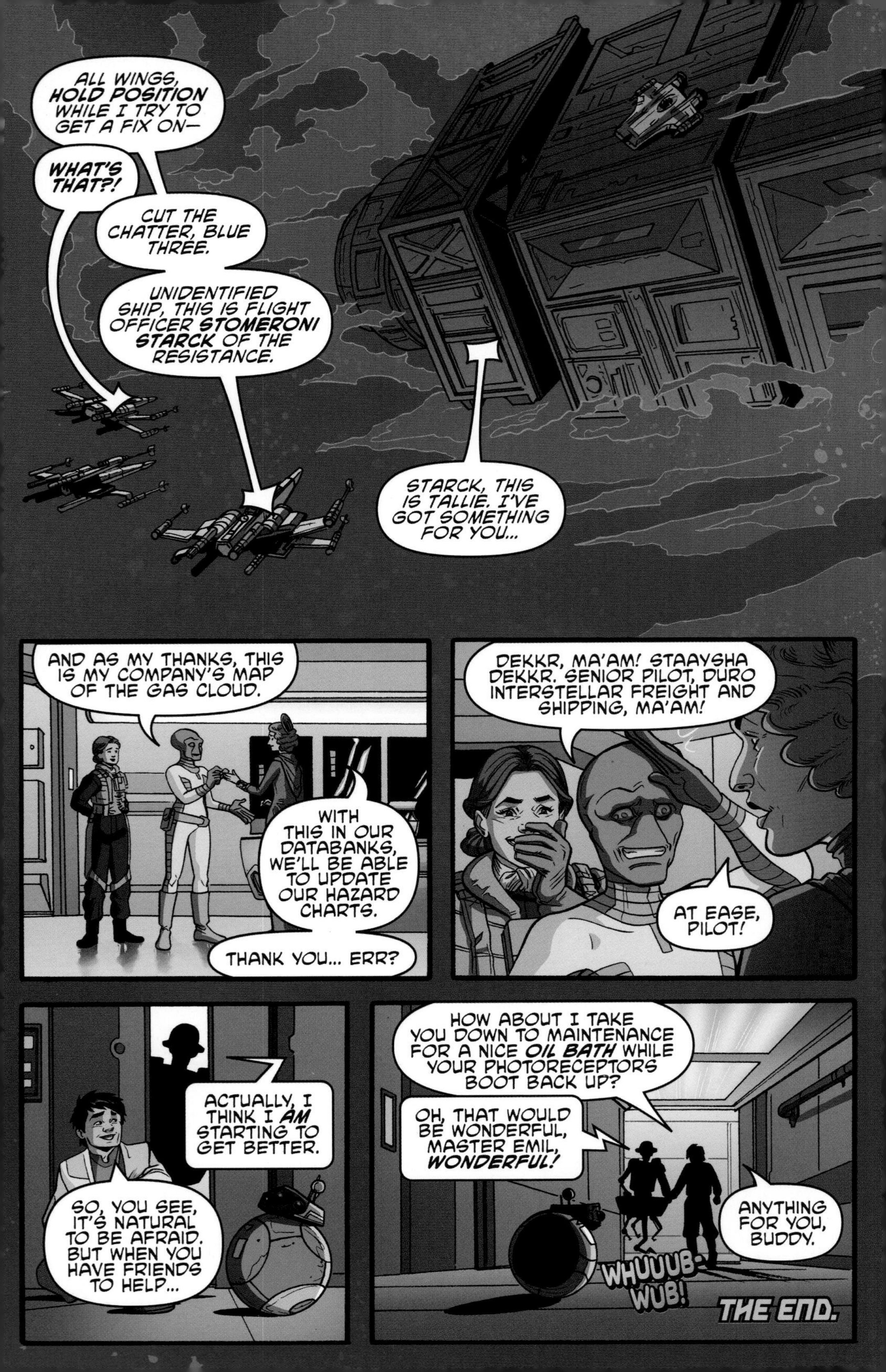
ALL WINGS, HOLD POSITION WHILE I TRY TO GET A FIX ON—
WHAT'S THAT?!
CUT THE CHATTER, BLUE THREE.
UNIDENTIFIED SHIP, THIS IS FLIGHT OFFICER STOMERONI STARCK OF THE RESISTANCE.
STARCK, THIS IS TALLIE. I'VE GOT SOMETHING FOR YOU...
AND AS MY THANKS, THIS IS MY COMPANY'S MAP OF THE GAS CLOUD.
WITH THIS IN OUR DATABANKS, WE'LL BE ABLE TO UPDATE OUR HAZARD CHARTS.
THANK YOU... ERR?
DEKKR, MA'AM! STAAYSHA DEKKR. SENIOR PILOT, DURO INTERSTELLAR FREIGHT AND SHIPPING, MA'AM!
AT EASE, PILOT!
SO, YOU SEE, IT'S NATURAL TO BE AFRAID. BUT WHEN YOU HAVE FRIENDS TO HELP...
ACTUALLY, I THINK I AM STARTING TO GET BETTER.
HOW ABOUT I TAKE YOU DOWN TO MAINTENANCE FOR A NICE OIL BATH WHILE YOUR PHOTORECEPTORS BOOT BACK UP?
OH, THAT WOULD BE WONDERFUL, MASTER EMIL, WONDERFUL!
ANYTHING FOR YOU, BUDDY.
WHUUUB-WUB!
THE END.

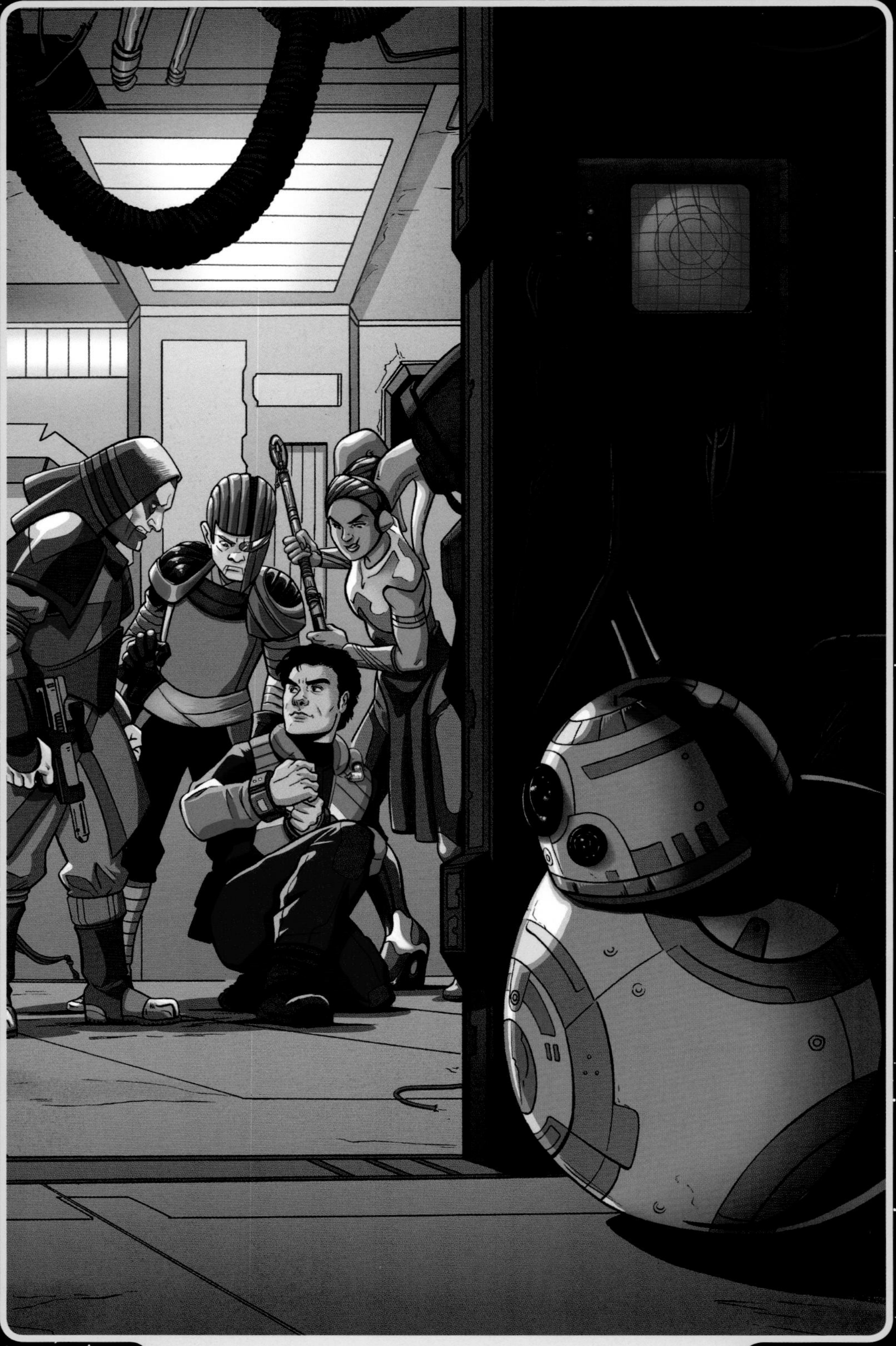

Art by Megan Levens, Colors by Charlie Kirchoff

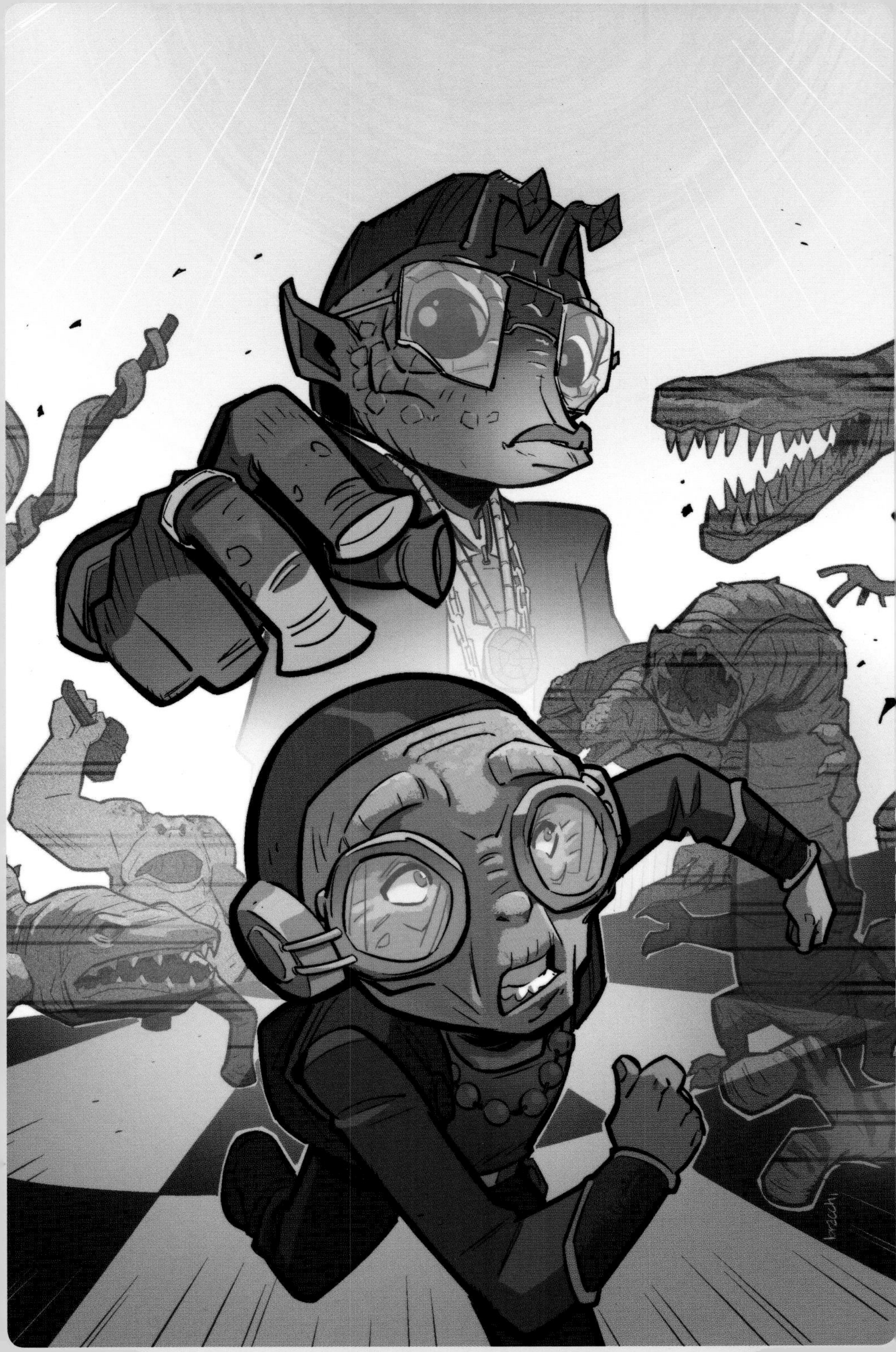

Art by Manuel Bracchi, Colors by Matt Herms

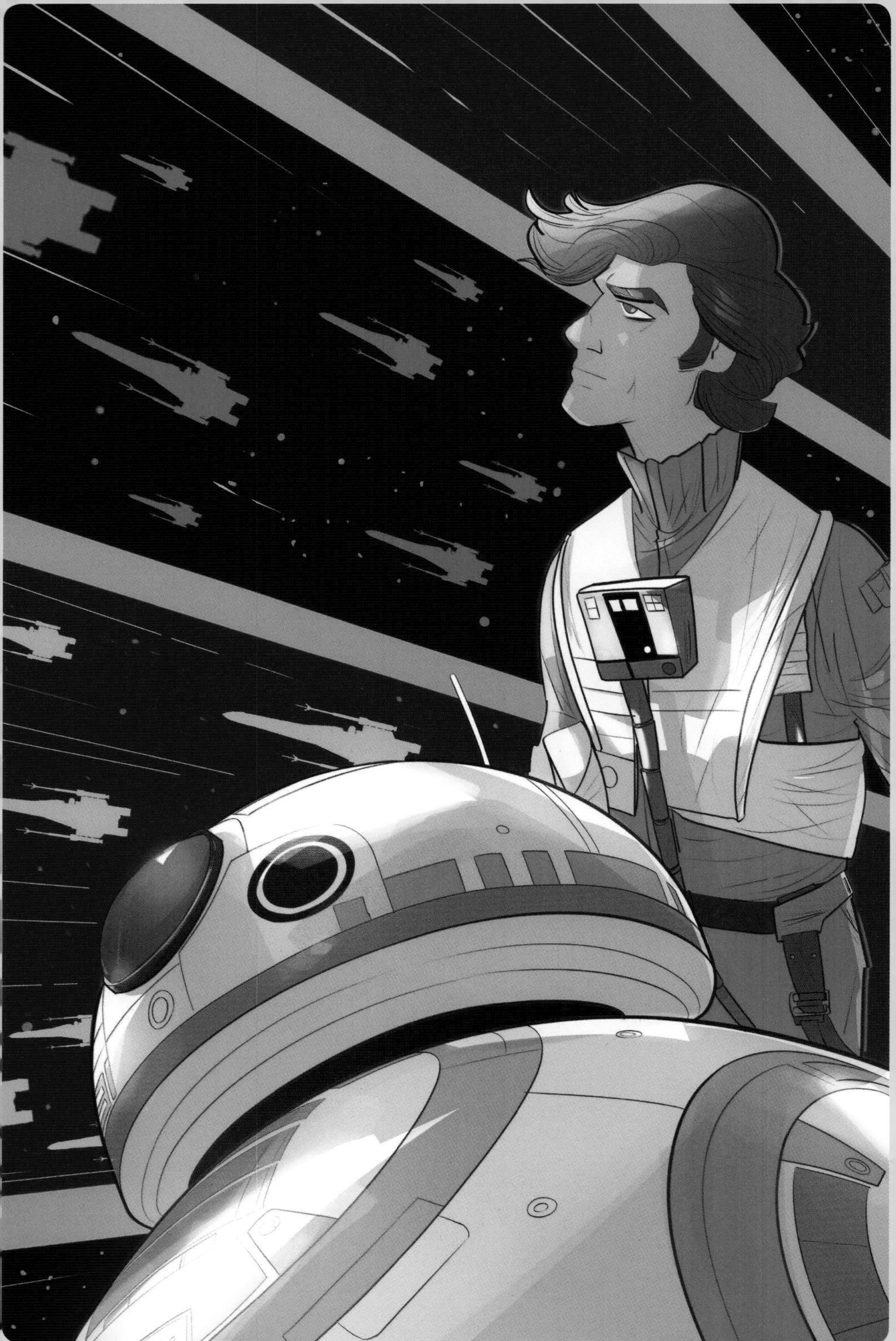

Art by Stefano Simeone

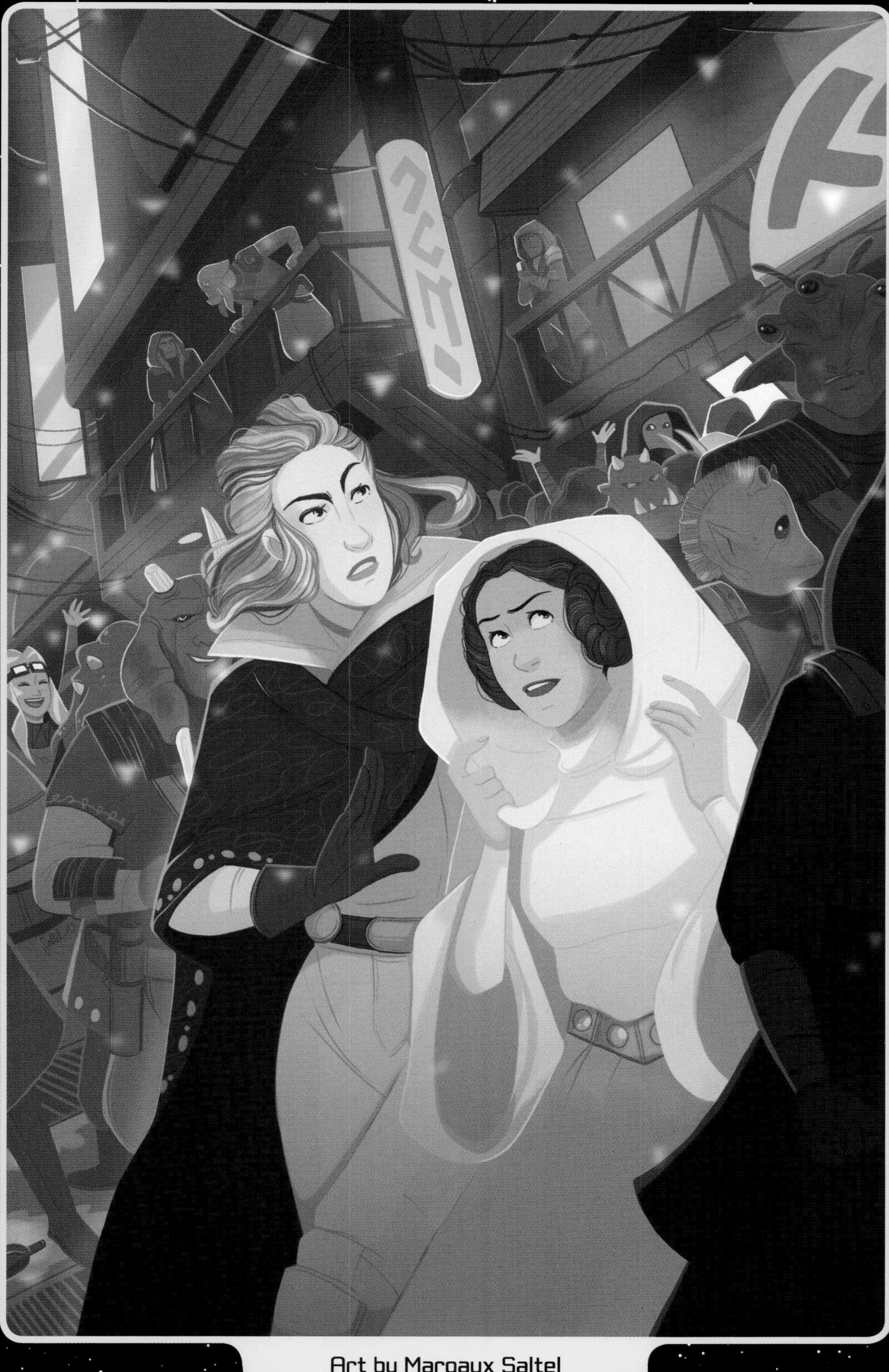

Art by Margaux Saltel

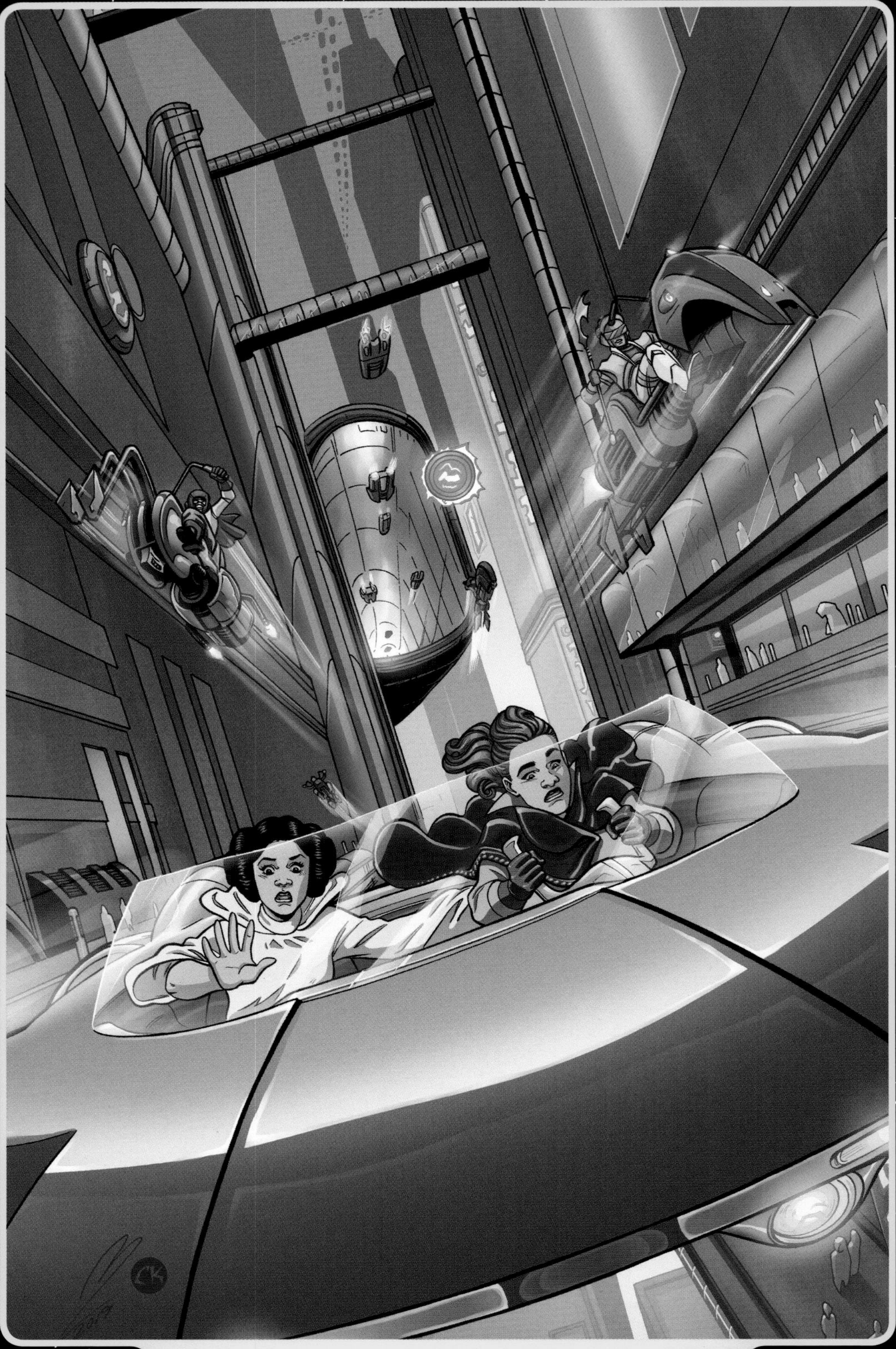

Art by Megan Levens, Colors by Charlie Kirchoff

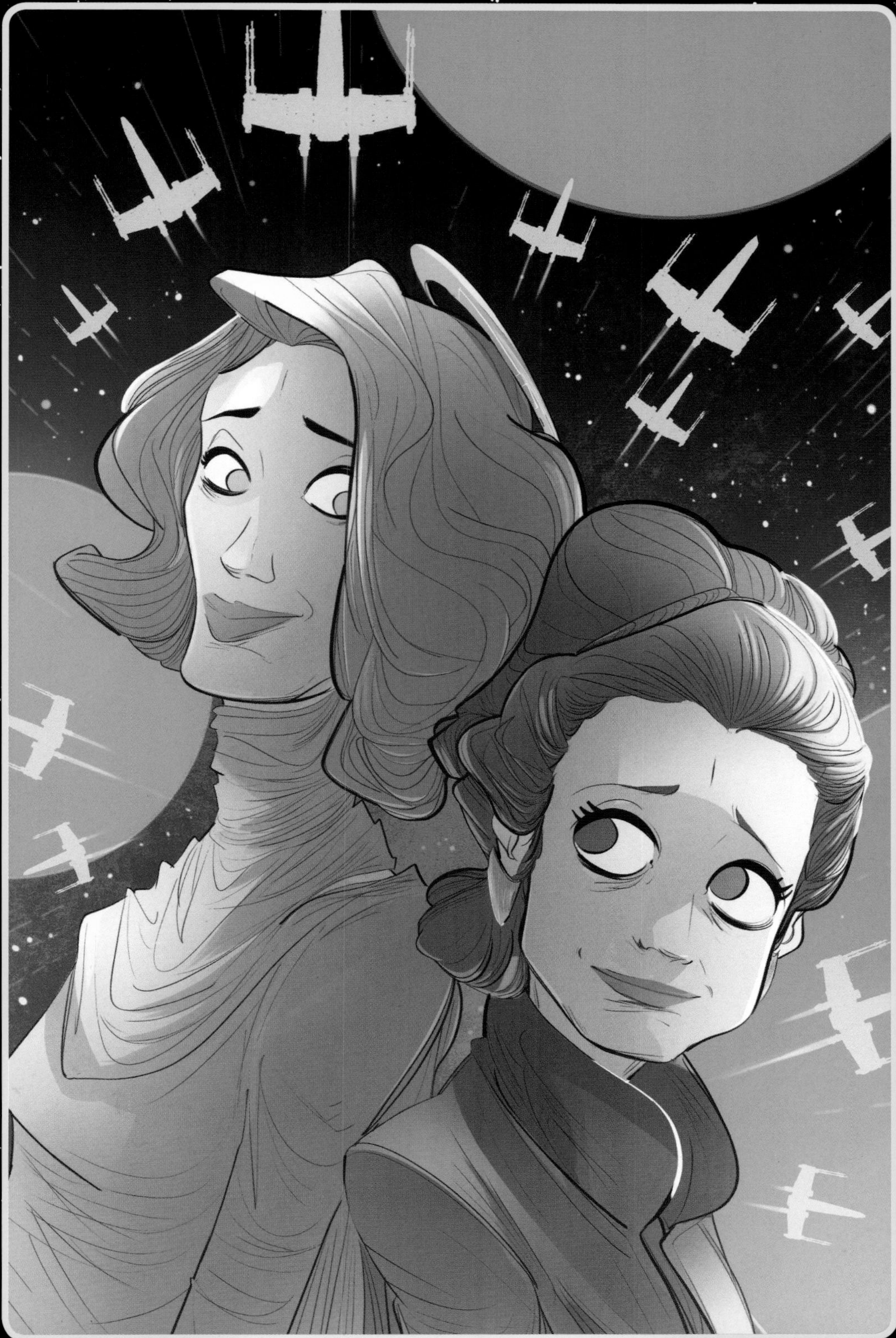

Art by Stefano Simeone

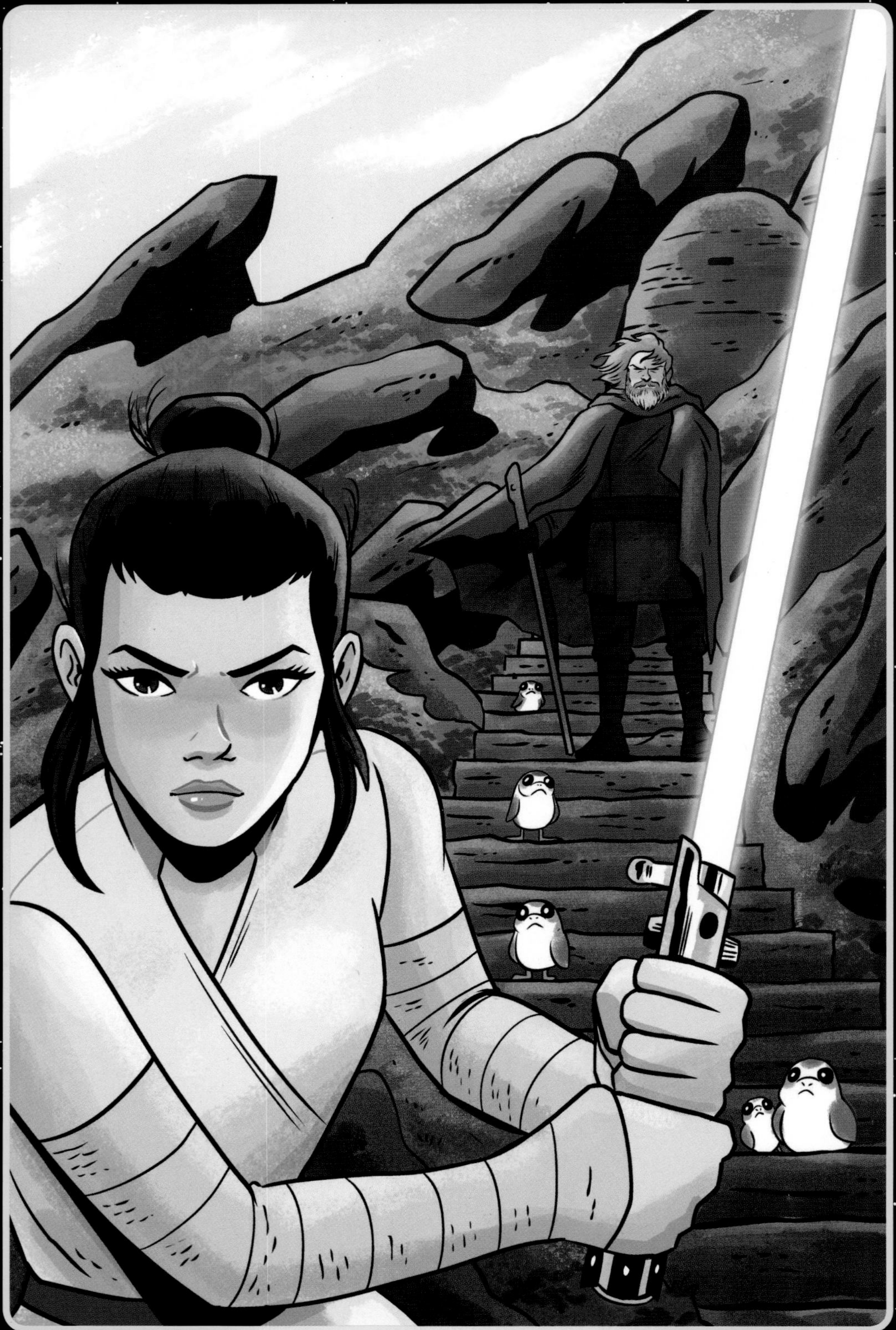

Art by Derek Charm

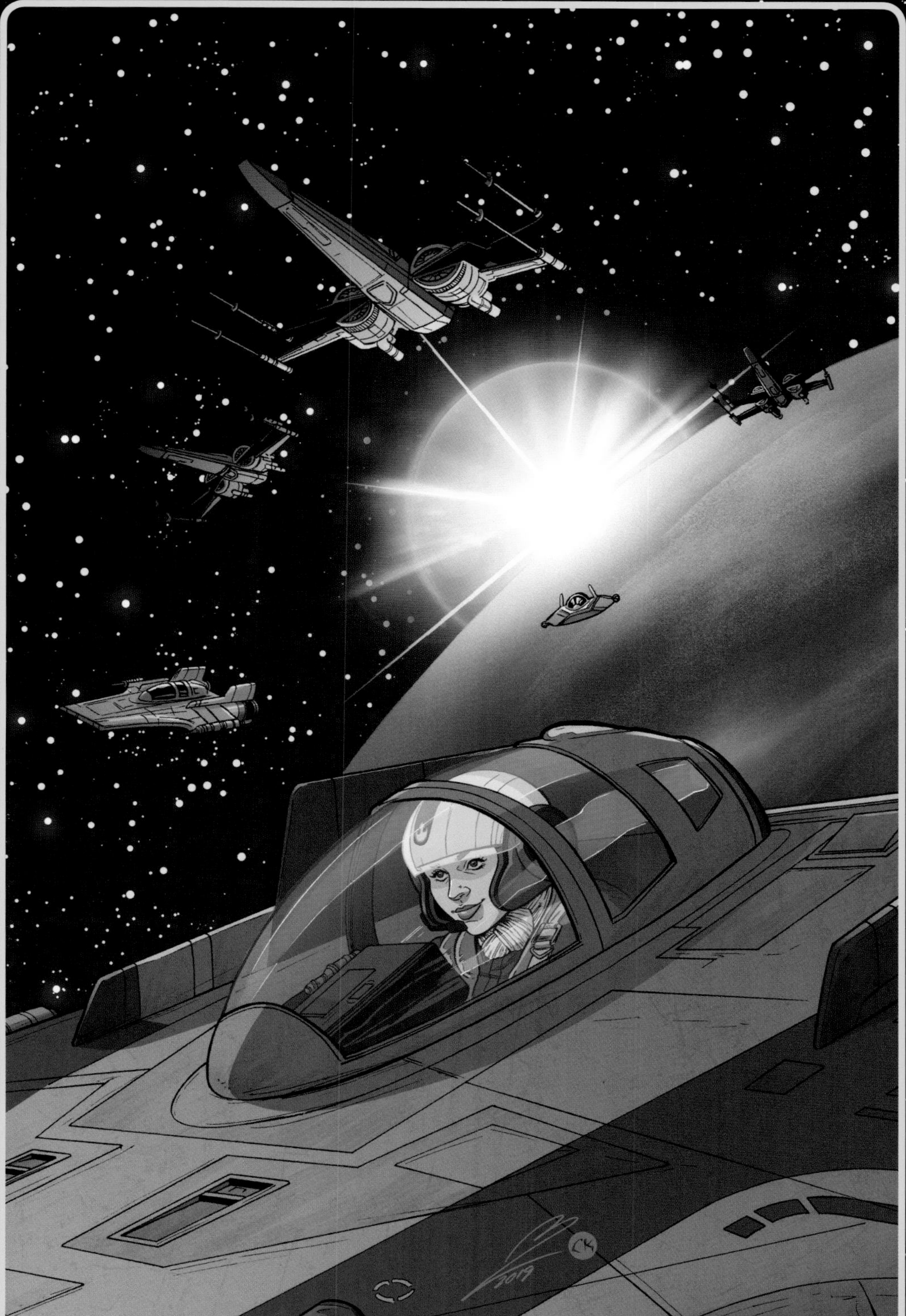

Art by Megan Levens, Colors by Charlie Kirchoff

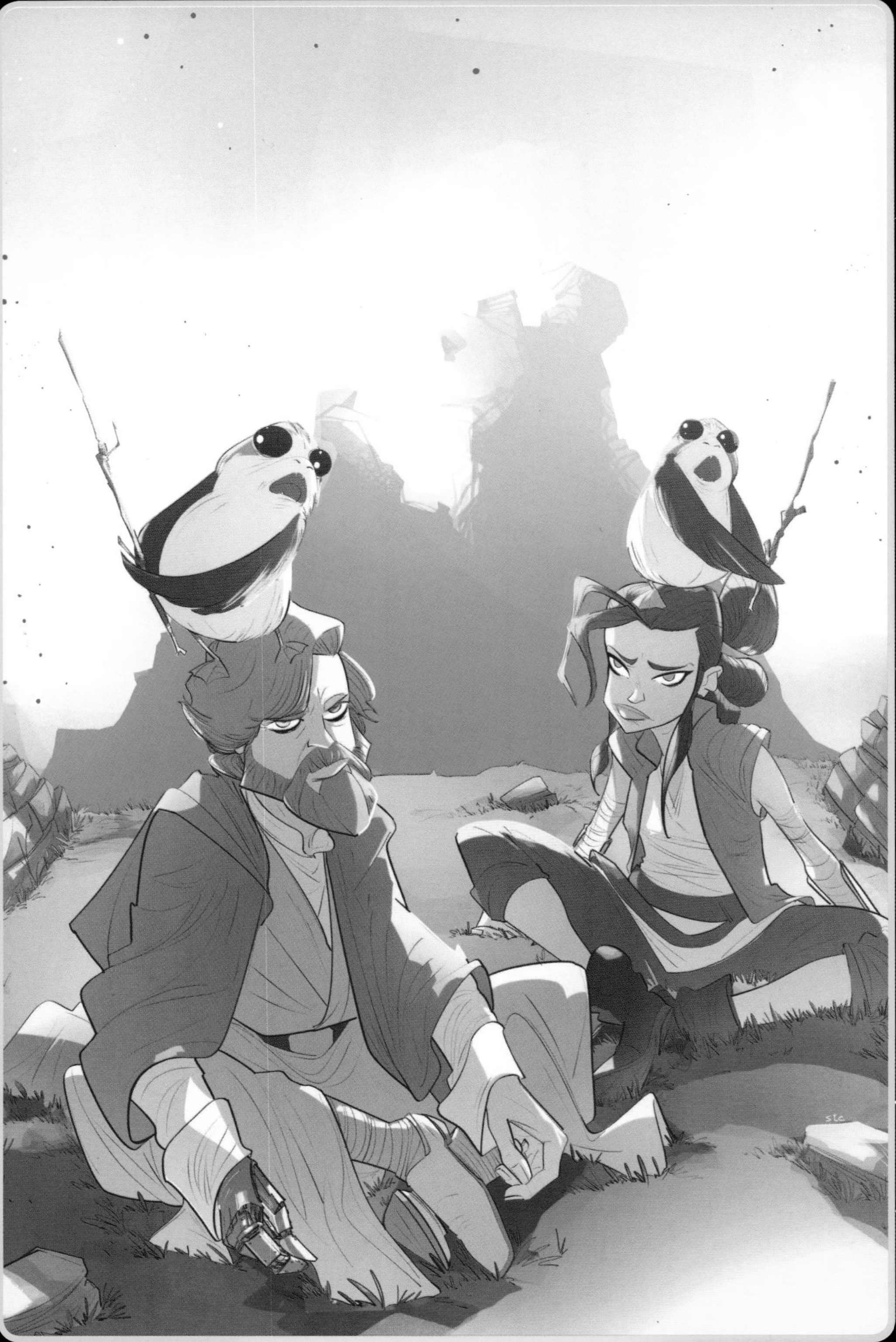

Art by Stefano Simeone

AMILYN HOLDO

An unconventional Resistance officer, Amilyn Holdo was one of Leia Organa's oldest friends. She assumed command of the Resistance fleet after Leia was injured. As the peril to the Resistance grew, Holdo's insistence on secrecy and her brusque manner led her into conflict with Poe Dameron. She sacrificed her life to save the Resistance transports during the desperate flight to Crait.

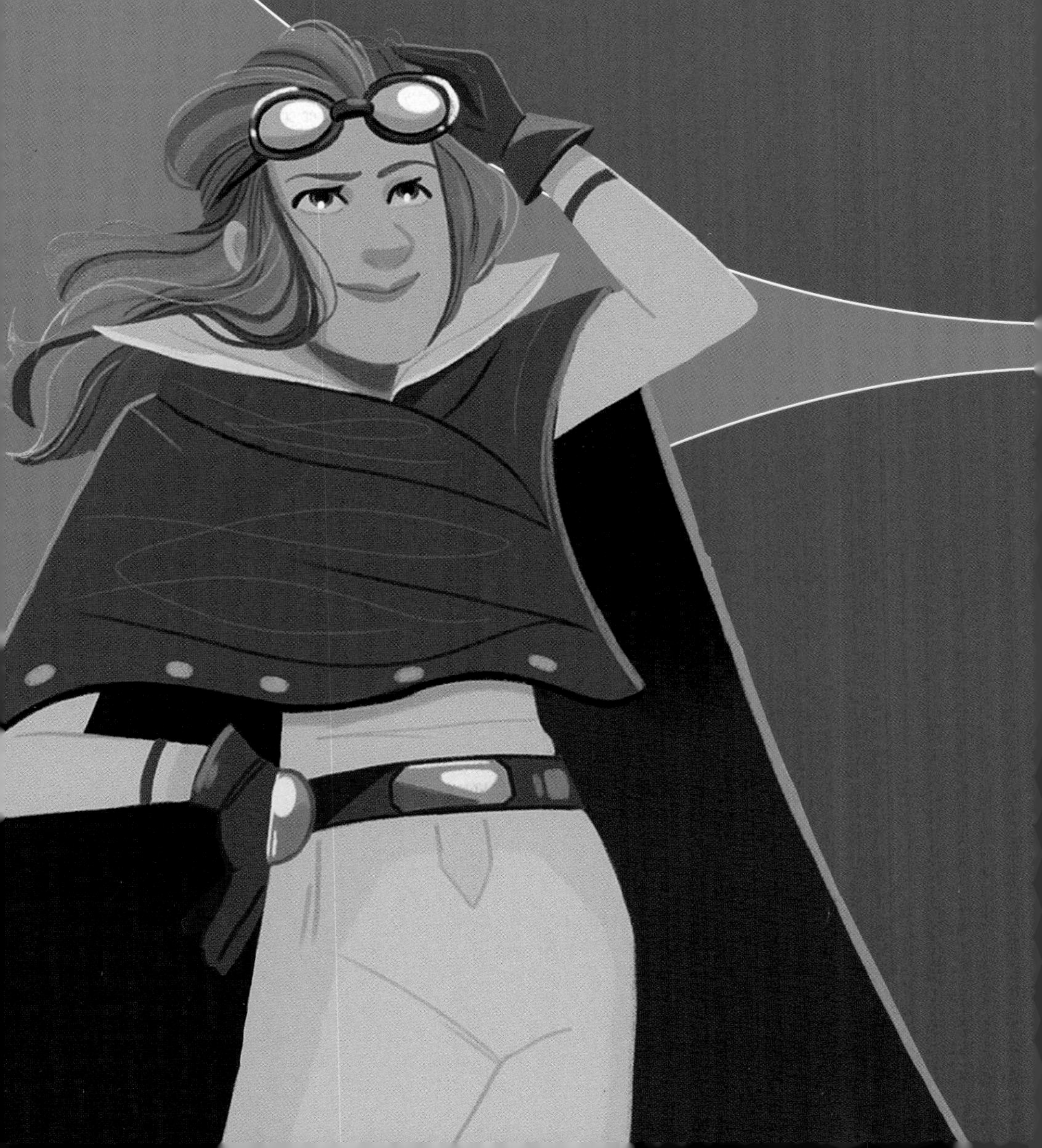

MAZ KANATA

Maz Kanata is more than a thousand years old, a diminutive being with vast experience at surviving in the underworld. From her castle on Takodana, Maz has seen galactic powers rise and fall and felt the Force ebb and flow, seeking an elusive balance between darkness and light. She has given many a young smuggler a start by offering credits, equipment, or connections, and helped many an old friend rediscover a lost path.

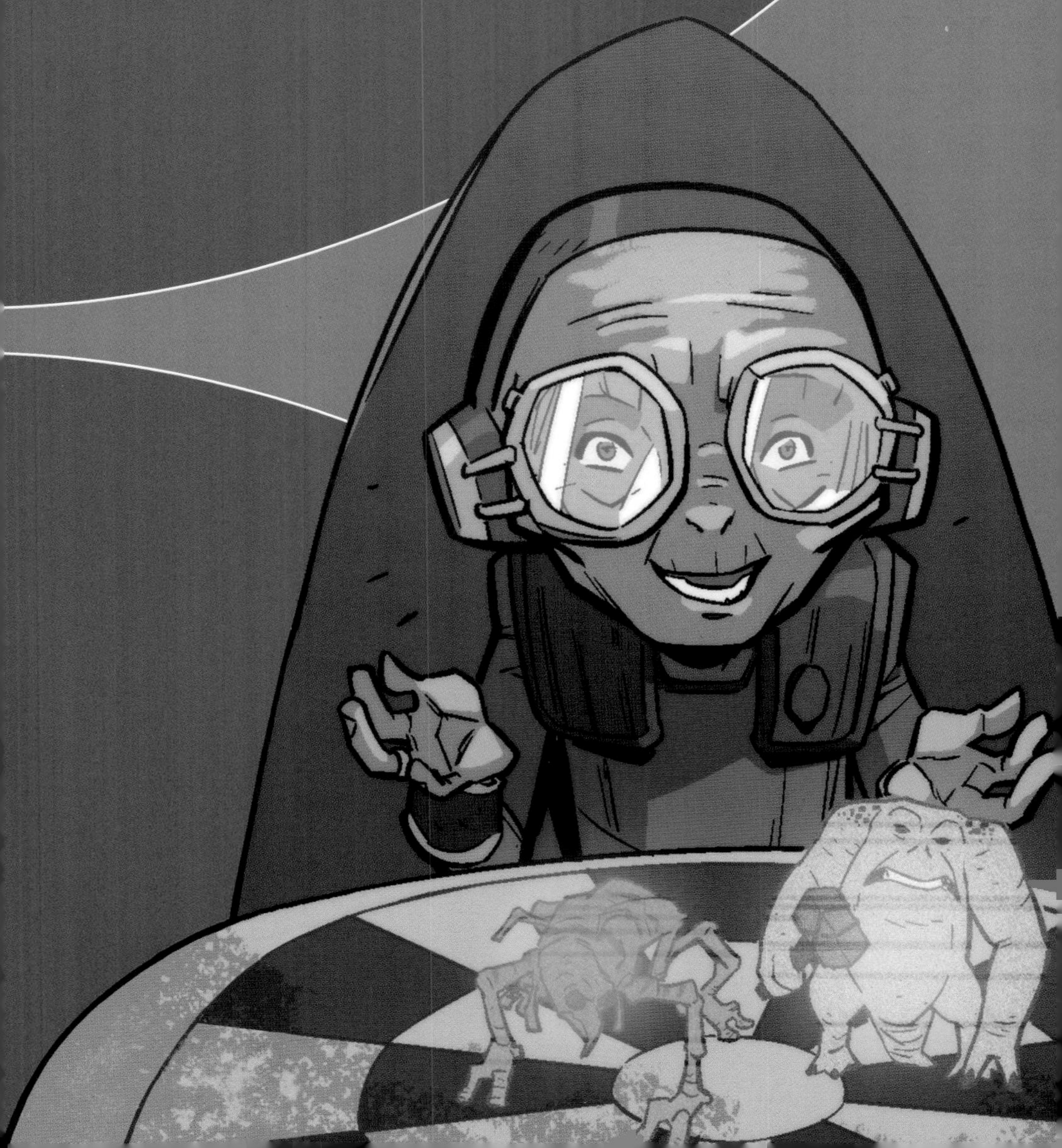

TALLIE LINTRA

Hailing from Pippip 3, young Lt. Tallissan Lintra was one of the Resistance's best pilots, impressing even Poe Dameron with her flying skills. Tallie led a hastily assembled squadron of A-wings and X-wings above D'Qar, protecting the Resistance's vulnerable bombers on their attack run against a First Order Siege Dreadnought. Tallie died when Kylo Ren blasted the main hangar of the Raddus with missiles.

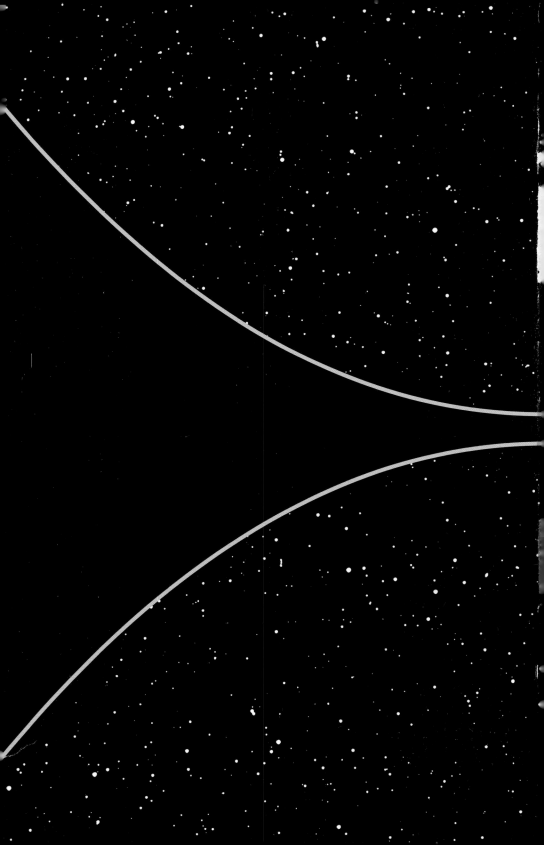